IN THE MIST

ARKHAM HOUSE FANTASY AND SCIENCE FICTION

IN THE MIST

and other uncanny encounters

Elizabeth Walter

Frontispiece by Stephen E. Fabian

ARKHAM HOUSE / 1979

Library of Congress Cataloging in Publication Data

Walter, Elizabeth.
   In the mist, and other uncanny encounters.

   CONTENTS: The concrete captain. — The sin eater. —
In the mist. [etc.]
   I. Title.
PZ4.W23In   1979   [PR6073.A4285]   823′.9′14   78-58752
ISBN 0-87054-083-1

Printed in the United States of America

CONTENTS

PREFACE

I was born interested in the supernatural. It is the only explanation I can offer of why I have been convinced for as long as I can remember that there is a world beyond the usual limits of our consciousness — the world next door. I have also written short stories for as long as I can remember, and at some point the two interests coalesced. I cannot now recall my first supernatural story, but it was certainly written in my early teens.

People often ask if I do not find it frightening, writing about the supernatural in the lonely small hours of the night. The answer is no. It is the unknown that is frightening — and I am not venturing into the unknown. Of course I hope to give my readers some chilling surprises, but they are surprises I have planned. Indeed, I often write the last line of a story first and then work towards it, once I have got the basic situation and characters right.

Settings to me are vitally important. They give solidity, reality. It is not difficult to imagine a shadowy figure gliding among moonlit ruins; it is less easy (but far more unnerving) if the setting is a suburban flat. Atmospheric conditions are also important in my

stories. The sea in all its moods, wind, snow, mist and darkness —
these are the things I love. They can give a fantastic twist to the most
familiar landscapes and objects — a parallel to what I like to do with
ideas. And since madness is sometimes no more than an unexpected
angle of vision, that too can play a part.

Some years ago in Cornwall, where the coast is rocky, the seas
treacherous, and wrecks common, I read with fascination of the
burial in the early years of this century of the captain of a vessel lost
in a storm. He had become wedged so firmly between two rocks that
it was impossible to release his body, so he was encased in concrete
and the burial service read over the result. After another tremendous
storm some years later the block of concrete was found to have
disappeared . . . the sea presumably reclaimed him. My imagination
did the rest in the first story in this collection, "The Concrete
Captain."

The custom of sin-eating, which provides the title for "The Sin-
Eater," is peculiar to the Welsh Border where I come from, though
no longer practised there. The seventeenth-century antiquary John
Aubrey gives an excellent account of it in his *Remaines of Gentilisme
and Judaisme:*

> In the County of Hereford was an old Custome at funeralls to have poor
> people, who were to take upon them all the sinnes of the party
> deceased. One of them I remember lived in a cottage on Rosse high-
> way. He was a long leane, ugly, lamentable poor raskel. The Manner
> was that when the Corps was brought out of the house and layd on the
> Biere, a Loafe of bread was brought out and delivered to the Sinne-
> eater over the corps, as also a Mazer-bowle of maple full of beer, which
> he was to drinke up, and sixpence in money, in consideration whereof
> he took upon him ipso facto all the Sinnes of the Defunct, and freed
> him (or her) from walking after they were dead. . . .

No one knows when the custom died out. When I first mentioned it,
my grandmother claimed to have heard of it, but she had no clear
idea of what it was. I found myself wondering what a sin-eater would
feel if, after accepting the sins of the dead man, he discovered that he
had taken on more than he knew.

The circumstances surrounding the title-story in this volume occurred a few years ago when I visited Eastern England — particularly the counties of Lincolnshire and Yorkshire — to see the marvellous cathedrals and ruined abbeys there. To my surprise, I found that what lingered most in my mind was not the glory of Gothic and Romanesque, but the wartime connection of this part of England with the RAF and USAAF. Most of the big bomber bases were here. There are still traces of them among the fields, and it is impossible to stand in the RAF Memorial Chapel in Lincoln Cathedral and not be deeply moved. I also had the experience of being caught briefly in fog on the Yorkshire Moors, and very eerie it was. "In the Mist" was born out of that experience, and is in some small way a tribute to all the men from those air force bases who did not make it home.

I owe the story "Come and Get Me" to a friend, who told me how she had once visited a derelict house in North Wales and been so overcome by an atmosphere of evil emanating from it that she took to her heels, pursued by mocking laughter. Of course I said it was a woodpecker she heard, but I am by no means certain. . . . Anyway, I decided to use it as the basis of a story, and since I do not know North Wales, I transferred it to the Elan Valley in South Wales, which I know well.

The parrot in this tale I owe in part to another friend, who had a talking budgerigar which had been taught to speak by her late mother. She one day confessed to me that she found it very unnerving to hear the bird say, "Polly, put the kettle on," in her dead mother's voice. The budgerigar became a parrot because one of my earliest memories is of being allowed to visit an African grey parrot belonging to some neighbours. I can see him now, hunched in his cage on a low table at child level, drawing down a grey, wrinkled, reptilian eyelid in boredom. But when I put a finger through the bars of his cage, I discovered that he could move like lightning and that he had a very hard beak! I have always owed him a nip in return, and offer it through this story with nearly half a century of interest.

"The Island of Regrets" too I owe to a friend, who vividly

described how he had visited an island off the coast of Brittany and the sudden shock of coming unexpectedly on the deserted house at its heart and wondering what its history might be. This work also contains two other favourite themes of mine: the fairy-tale element of the wish which comes true in the one way you don't want it to (used so brilliantly by W. W. Jacobs in "The Monkey's Paw"), and the close relationship between sanity and madness.

"The Hare" comes straight from my own experience. This creature is traditionally associated with witches and there are legends in many countries about witches who could change themselves into hares at will. Witchcraft is also particularly associated with the Harz Mountains in Germany, where this story is set. The Brocken, the highest mountain in the Harz, is the scene of the traditional Walpurgisnacht gathering of witches on April thirtieth (May Eve), when they are said to sweep away the last of the snow with their brooms. But now the Harz Mountains are divided by the frontier between East and West Germany, which cuts through them. One can see, but not visit, the Brocken from the West, and the tragedy of a divided country and totally artificial frontier made a deep impression on me when I visited the Harz. While I was out walking one day in the woods, a huge hare bounded away from under my feet, exactly as I have described. I looked at its full, dark, inscrutable, and not at all frightened eye, and knew that I would someday write a story about it, of which "The Hare" is the result.

The concluding work in this volume and the favourite among all my stories is "Davy Jones's Tale." The setting is the extreme south-west tip of Wales — Pembrokeshire — which juts out into the Atlantic Ocean with no land between it and America. The coastline is beautiful — a treasury of wild flowers, seals, and bird life. It is also a treacherous coast, with pounding surf, sheer cliffs, sandy bays with vicious undertows, and a long and doleful record of wrecks in the days of sail.

I read with interest an account of how a lifeboat-station had had to be moved in the nineteenth century because on one occasion the lifeboatmen were unable to row their boat beyond the harbour-bar on account of a strong south-west gale blowing onshore. As a result, a ship was lost with all hands. The story haunted me. It still does, and it is one of the few stories I have written which I can still reread with pleasure. Perhaps it will haunt you too.

ELIZABETH WALTER

London, England
21 March 1978

THE CONCRETE CAPTAIN

NTIL A FEW YEARS AGO THE ROCK CALLED "THE CAPTAIN" WAS A landmark in the South Cornish fishing village of Nancarrow. It was a curiously smooth rock, covered with long greenish weed like hair instead of the bladder-wrack which clung to its more rugged companions, and it lay at an angle quite contrary to the usual inclination of the coast dictated by centuries of winds and tides. The fishermen superstitiously bared their heads to it when passing, and after Nancarrow began to be taken over by the tourists, the custom caught on and everyone else did too, without seeking to know any more about it than that it was a local tradition which it seemed better to observe.

Jeremy Sparrow was the exception. For one thing he was a journalist, that is, someone paid to be curious about his surroundings; for another, he was an expert boatman himself. He hired a small motor launch when he came to Nancarrow on holiday, and puttered round the coast with such obvious skill and intelligence that old Bert Tanner, who had leased him the boat, began to think his insurance premiums were too high.

But it was not until his third visit that Jeremy became curious about the Captain, and then it was mainly by chance. He had sailed rather nearer to the rock formation than he had intended, and though he was no geologist, he couldn't help noticing certain features about the rocks that were not apparent at a distance. He asked questions that night in his hotel.

The Smugglers' Rest, which had no association with smuggling, but did its best by means of artificially low ceilings, ships' lanterns, and bow windows with bottle-glass carefully inserted, to look as though it might once have had, was not particularly full in early June. Even so, Jeremy's question was quickly side-stepped before it could be overheard.

"You're right, Mr. Sparrow," the barman said confidentially, "that rock's a block of concrete. Got wedged there after a big storm. But we don't generally let on to visitors — it spoils the story, you see."

"Story?" Jeremy's journalist pulses quickened.

"We-ell, folks can make of it what they like."

"But I've never heard any story."

"Why, come to that, neither have I — beyond what I say: the lump were washed up after a gigantic storm in these parts, and wedged between those rocks."

"How long ago?"

"Before I was born, I can tell 'ee."

Jeremy calculated. "That's at least fifty years ago."

The barman laughed with delighted uneasiness. "Near enough, Mr. Sparrow, near enough."

"And you mean to say that's all there is to it? What was the concrete for?"

"Ballast maybe, or broke off from somebody's quayside."

"Unlikely," Jeremy said. "Besides, it's a very funny shape when you look at it."

"Can't say as I ever have."

"Come on, Will, that's no answer and you know it."

"Well, the seas have been pounding it, you see."

"They've pounded it smooth, but it must have been oblong to start with, and between five and six feet long."

"Five feet ten and three-quarter inches."

"Not bad for a man who's never looked at it."

Will Trelean retracted quickly. "Everyone knows that round here."

"And why should the exact dimensions of this block of concrete be so significant? I'm certain there's a story there. Come to that, why do you all salute it in passing, and how did it get its name?"

Will looked desperately around, but no help was forthcoming. The other visitors to his bar were busy swapping fishing stories with the locals, which at least meant they hadn't overheard.

"I suppose it's called the Captain because it's about the height of a man," he hazarded.

"That doesn't explain why you bare your heads."

"I don't know. You'd best ask Parson."

"All right," Jeremy Sparrow said. "I will." He wondered very much what the Reverend Ian Phelps, a comparative newcomer to Nancarrow, could tell him that was unknown to Will Trelean, who had lived there all his life.

But Will had overlooked the fact that it was not so easy to have a word with Parson now that Nancarrow was one of three parishes which had been telescoped into one. Holy Communion and Matins were held in its church on the third Sunday of every month, and Evensong on the second, and the next Sunday of Jeremy Sparrow's visit was the fourth. Sooner than drive inland to Bodruan, where the Reverend Phelps was based, Jeremy made a point of having a word with Ned Jarvis when he next passed the old man's house.

Ned had been a fisherman all his life until a rough sea had trapped his leg between boat and quayside, and rheumatism had done the rest. He was past retiring age anyway, but without the sea he was more of a widower than he had been when he lost his wife. In fine weather he sat in the doorway of his cottage above the harbour, his stiff leg stuck out in front of him, mending nets, endlessly pipe-smoking, making shell boxes, and exchanging a word with everyone who passed by.

When Jeremy approached him for information, his first remark was, "Who's been telling you about the Captain?"

"I didn't know there was anything to tell." Jeremy tried to make the answer sound artless but Ned Jarvis was not deceived.

"Nobody'd want to know about that old block of concrete without he'd heard something," he declared.

"I haven't heard anything, only Will was so funny when I asked about it. He suggested I should ask Mr. Phelps."

"Parson?" Ned spat with force and accuracy. "What's he know, a newcomer like that?"

"Just what I thought," Jeremy said, delighted.

"Mind you, I can see why Will said it," Ned went on. "You've got to be careful when dealing with spirits."

"What have spirits to do with a block of concrete?"

Ned looked at him narrowly. "Don't you know? There's a dead man inside."

Of all the possible explanations which had run through his mind, this was not one which had occurred to Jeremy. He gazed thunderstruck at Ned Jarvis, who was clearly enjoying the effect produced.

"How can there be?" he said at last.

"We poured the concrete over him. My father did, that's to say. He and the other men of Nancarrow about the turn of the century."

"Why?"

"Because his body was trapped between those rocks so that they couldn't release him and it was putting them off their crab teas."

"Hadn't you better tell me the whole story?"

"It's not much of a story to tell."

Nevertheless, Ned was only too willing to embark on it. The brig *Ottawa,* bound for Cork in midwinter, had put into Falmouth for orders and had been wrecked off Nancarrow in a storm. The seas were such that no one could get near her, although she was not fifty yards offshore. Several of the crew were washed overboard; the rest clung to the rigging as she listed more and more to port. At length one man — they learnt later he was the Captain, "a big powerful fellow," said Ned — seizing what he judged a favourable moment, endeavoured to swim ashore. He got so close that the watchers who had run down the rocks to meet him, at considerable risk to themselves, could see the swell of his muscles as his arms clove through the water and he surfaced time and again, shaking his mighty head. But the wind had veered and the tide was running against him. Try as he might he could make no headway in that sea. The threshing of his arms grew weaker, he surfaced less often, until he was submerged by a wave bigger than its companions, and lost to sight in a wild waste of sea. When morning came there were no men left clinging to the rigging, though their bodies were washed ashore. But not until three days later, when the storm had abated, was the Captain's body found.

He was caught fast between two rocks and wedged so firmly that all efforts to release him failed. Since he could not be given Christian burial and since the people of Nancarrow could not endure the sight of him, for his body was exposed at low tide, they got permission to bury him in concrete, and this was duly done, forming a solid block the exact height of the Captain over which the vicar read the burial service.

"And that ought to have been the end of him," Ned Jarvis concluded. "You couldn't have anything more Christian than that. But it seemed like he weren't satisfied, and when a storm's coming he cries out."

"Cries out?"

"Ay, there's many here has heard him, but don't ask me what he says, for some says one thing and some another. One man even heard his own name.

"Yes, my brother Samuel that was, though mark you, I've said nought of this till now. And it were partly Sam's fault, I reckon. He were like you: he wouldn't bare his head. Said it were a silly custom, as I don't mind admitting it is. Still, there's such a thing as respect for a dead man, especially when he doesn't lie easy, and Sam ought to have knowed it, you see."

Jeremy accepted the implied rebuke in silence, and merely asked, "What happened then?"

"One evening," Ned resumed, "Sam was returning from a day's

fishing when he heard the Captain crying out, 'And sure as I stand here, Ned,' he told me, 'he was calling "Sam Jarvis," just like that. I heard it on the wind: "Sam Ja-arvis." I tell you it sent a shudder down my spine.' I told Sam he should treat it as a warning, but he wouldn't be warned by me, nor by the Captain neither. He insisted on going out just the same. Next day, of course, the weather worsened and the fishing fleet had to run for port. Most of us put in to Mevagissey, but Sam — well, he didn't make it, that's all."

"Have others heard their names called?"

"Not as I know of. Some say he calls the names of his crew, those in the churchyard and those on the ocean bottom, as though he wants to be in one or the other place. 'Tis neither one thing nor the other where he lies. They say Parson didn't rightly know what to say when he read the burial service; he couldn't commit him to the deep, when he was cased in concrete. I reckon he just hurried over that bit."

"And you never told anyone about your brother?"

"What good would it have done? Besides, Sam might have been mistaken — only I never got another chance to ask him. It's not happened again and it's more than forty years since Sam was lost. All the same, it can't hurt to be respectful. It's no joke for a man, being dead."

Once again, Jeremy chose not to answer, and changed the subject instead.

"But in Nancarrow you still don't like visitors to know about the Captain?"

Ned grinned. "Bad luck for the tourist trade. You can bet your life that was what Will Trelean was thinking. He didn't want to scare you away."

Yet recalling the barman's voice, Jeremy had the distinct impression that it was Will Trelean who had been scared.

Jeremy had an unexpected opportunity to make the closer acquaintance of the Captain when he set out to sail up the coast next day. It was stiflingly hot, yet there was no hint of thunder. And then, at the harbour mouth, his engine stalled. It took only a moment to restart it, but in that time the ebb tide had carried him slightly towards the Captain, and Jeremy resolved to make the most of his chance. Leaving the engine switched off, he allowed his boat to drift as the tide dictated while he leaned on the engine house and looked out.

He could see the barnacles encrusting the lower half of the Captain; he could see the concrete's pitted surface and green weed; a long trail of sand-coloured ribbon-weed had become entangled, and floated on the water like a cravat. The lower half of the block was still submerged, and no doubt it was the movement of the water, but it seemed to Jeremy that the concrete tilted slightly towards him as if in salutation. He defiantly refused to bow back.

If his eyes were playing tricks upon him, it seemed that his ears were the next to do so, for he distinctly heard the concrete give a long-drawn-out wailing cry. It was exactly the sound that might have been produced by rock grating on concrete, and Jeremy was interested chiefly because here was the scientific explanation of the sound which Sam Jarvis and others had heard. It was also proof that his eyes had not deceived him, that the Captain had indeed moved. What defied explanation was the force responsible, for the sea was calm and clear as a vast rock pool.

Jeremy was toying with elementary physics—fulcrum, leverage of its own weight, and the like—when the block cried out again, several short notes and a long one. He began to think it had an eerie sound. The whole business filled him with the same uneasiness he had felt at a table-turning session he had attended long ago. In the absence of a natural explanation one was forced back on the supernatural—and Jeremy had a finite, logical mind.

Or at least he thought he had, but he rapidly began to doubt it, for next moment he could have sworn he heard his own name. The three short notes and a long one were repeated, and cried "Jeremy Spa-arrow" for all the world to hear.

Jeremy felt his skin prickle with agitation. The Captain was calling him, as he cried out to his drowned crew to join him, as he had called Sam Jarvis forty years ago. Then he took a grip on himself. It was all nonsense, inspired by the yarn Ned Jarvis had spun him. In any case, there was no sign of a tempest, and the weather forecast indicated set fair. In these latitudes squalls did not blow up suddenly from nowhere, and if the sea turned choppy there were innumerable harbours along the South Cornish coast. It would be absurd to give up a day's sailing because of a superstitious whim, because of a sound for which there was a natural explanation in the grinding of concrete on rock.

Jeremy was not going to be put off by so-called supernatural manifestations. He started his engine into life and went puttering off round the headland without giving the Captain a further thought.

The sea was so calm that after lunch Jeremy cast anchor, and stretched out full length on deck. He was close inshore, but the cliffs, even at this distance, were blue and hazy with heat. The rocking of the boat was more soothing than a cradle. In no time he was fast asleep.

He awoke because it had turned colder. The sun had suddenly gone in. The coast was still a blue, but it was darker, while out to sea . . . Out to sea there was nothing but whiteness, undifferentiated between sea and sky; not the pure candid whiteness of light, brilliant and translucent, but utter neutrality. No forms, no colours, no movement, except its inevitable approach. It was one of the thickest sea fogs Jeremy could ever remember. He started up his engine in haste.

It was necessary to put out to sea to round the next headland and avoid the rocks close inshore, but once past that, there was an excellent harbour at no great distance. He should be safe enough. The boat chugged on towards the wall of whiteness, her nose pointed towards the open sea. One moment he could see it approaching and the next it was all about him, making him shiver with cold.

Jeremy reduced speed and put on a thick sweater. His world had grown very small, the world of a motor launch surrounded on all sides by walls of silence, even the chugging of her engine muffled and faint. Then that noise too ceased on the instant Jeremy tried vainly to start her again, but all seemed in order; oil and fuel were sufficient, there was no obvious mechanical fault. She had stalled, just as she had stalled when passing the Captain, and for as little apparent cause. If this were the meaning of the Captain's warning then he had indeed been a fool not to heed it, Jeremy ruefully admitted to himself.

He might as well have been under canvas, for all the headway he could make. Even so, he was not particularly worried. He was becalmed, but that was all. The mist would probably lift in the evening, when a land breeze started up. Meanwhile he was safely out of the path of other vessels. He needed only patience.

He soon found that other qualities were required of him, such as an iron control of his nerves. It was all too easy to imagine unpleasant occurrences, such as drifting onto unexpected rocks. The damp chill of the mist was all about him. His hair was already wringing wet. Beads of moisture clung to his thick sweater. Even the inside of the wheelhouse felt dank.

Jeremy had another go at starting the engine and checked again the things that might be wrong.

He reckoned himself a moderately good mechanic, and was both surprised and irritated to find himself beaten like this. He could feel no noticeable movement of the boat, but he could not go on drifting and perhaps be caught in some current and swept out to sea or carried onto the rocks. There was nothing for it but to cast anchor, curl up in the wheelhouse, and ride it out until the fog dispersed.

He was in the bows making ready to release the anchor when he heard a curious swishing sound. It came from ahead of him, and sounded as though a large object were cleaving through the water, and cleaving straight towards him too. Jeremy knew that sharks were sometimes caught in mid-Channel, but this sounded more like a whale. He peered intently into the whiteness, but it was as impenetrable as before. Then for a moment it parted. He had just time to see before him a high prow and to realize that he was experiencing the small boatman's nightmare of being run down in fog by a larger vessel off course.

Frantically Jeremy hauled in the anchor and seized the paddle. It was madness to hope he could get away. The paddle was never intended for anything more than pushing the boat off in harbour, or guiding her when drifting among rocks. And then it suddenly struck him that this strange vessel was heading straight towards the coast. She was going to run full tilt into the headland he had just rounded unless she altered course. Presumably she was out of control or unaware of her position to travel at such speed in fog. But what was driving her? He could not hear the throb of engines, yet she certainly was not drifting aimlessly. Whereas he was. Jeremy paddled frantically, but still the remorseless swishing sound came on. He had put on his life-jacket as a precaution, but he now anticipated he might actually need it. He was suddenly thankful there were no thrusting screws.

Then, as it seemed, only a few feet away from him, he saw the mysterious ship sweep by: she was a great three-masted sailing vessel, with all her canvas gone. She was running before a gale. Yet not a breath of wind was stirring. Sailors were clinging to her shrouds. On deck too men were grasping at handrails as though the seas were mountainous and all were bracing themselves as though in anticipation of a shock.

Jeremy waved and shouted, but it was as if he were not there. Or as if the mystery ship were a hallucination, something which only he could see. But its presence was real enough, to judge from the way the launch was behaving. It was bobbing like a cork in a rough sea. Caught up in the mighty wake as the sailing ship swept past him in a welter of threshing foam, Jeremy had neither breath nor strength to hail her. His own boat was being swamped. As fast as he baled out, another wave broke over her. He was thigh-deep in water and the launch was wallowing badly. Her engines certainly weren't going to be much good after this.

As he straightened momentarily between balings, Jeremy caught a last glimpse of the vessel's stern. The name *Ottawa* was painted upon it. Then it was lost in the mist.

It is probable that he would have been more frightened if he had been less preoccupied with keeping afloat. The vessel could not be a hallucination, for no hallucination would have left this turbulent wake. Nor would it have made that rending terrible crash of shivered timbers, and — with a report like gunshot — a mast snapped.

The sound was so loud, so close, so shattering, that Jeremy was almost deafened. The ship, like many another, had obviously run onto the rocks. Near him men might be drowning, dying, but all was hidden from view; and even if the fog lifted, without engines there was nothing he could do. Unless a few survivors managed to swim towards him. He could take one or two on board. But a ship that size must have a complement of upwards of a hundred. Among so many, what were one or two?

After the crash of the vessel striking the rocks there had been a deathly silence, the same fog-blanketed silence as before. The strange ship seemed to have come from nothing and returned to nothing. And then, in the midst of the silence, he heard a cry.

It was a lone voice, a man's, and it was coming towards him. Jeremy peered into the whiteness until his eyes ached, so that he was unprepared for a second cry, much nearer and coming from another direction. He spun round so fast he set the launch rocking again.

There, swimming, or rather battling towards him, was a man, his arms thrusting high out of the water as though he were contending with a heavy sea. His head turned from side to side, and his mouth shut and opened as he strove to gulp in air. But for all his efforts in a flat calm, he made little progress. And then Jeremy noticed another curious thing.

Where the man's legs should have been there was no movement either of water or of limbs. Perhaps he had been injured, crippled? Yet if so, how could he swim so powerfully?

Jeremy called out to him, but there was no answer. Was he a foreigner, perhaps? But the language of distress is international. The swimmer could have made some response. With all his strength Jeremy hurled the launch's lifebelt towards him. The swimmer took

no heed of it. On he came, slowly but with determination, towards
the little boat. Wedging himself firmly, Jeremy leaned over to help
him, felt the cold touch of the man's hand, the pull on his own
muscles as the stranger reached the launch and clung on. He hung
there motionless, too exhausted to make the last effort. The launch
had tilted alarmingly, surely more than it should with the man's
weight clinging to it. Jeremy leaned out as far as he dared to try and
get a grip on him and help him clamber aboard.

As he leaned over the side, he saw the inert legs more clearly. They
were greenish-grey and covered with hairlike weed. The lower half of
the man's body was encased in concrete and his weight was
threatening to capsize the boat.

"Let go!" Jeremy screamed. He had never known such panic. "Let
go!" he screamed again. And he hammered on the hands grasping
the gunwales. He glanced down at them. There was nothing there
but bone.

Seizing the paddle, he lifted it and brought it down with all his
might upon the clinging skeletal hands. He heard a bone crack, but
the grip did not loosen. About them, the white sea mist swirled. And
only one of them belonged to this world. The other belonged—who
knew where! Jeremy remembered Ned Jarvis saying that the Captain
was discontented, that he was buried neither on sea nor land and was
lonely in death with none of his crew around him. Was he seeking
company?

"What do you want?" Jeremy shouted, putting his face near the
Captain's own. "Tell me and I'll try to help you."

For answer the Captain raised his head. His lipless mouth opened
and gave forth a grating cry, such as rock might make grinding on
concrete. "Jeremy Spa-arrow," he said.

"No!" Jeremy cried. "You don't want me, I'm nothing to you. Go
away and leave me alone!"

The Captain heaved an arm over the side and more of him rose
from the water. Jeremy could see the barnacles encrusting his back.
Frantically he struck out with the paddle, but he might as well have
beaten on stone. With the first blow the paddle cracked and splin-

tered. The Captain did not even look up. His dark hair was plastered to his skull like seaweed. A trail of sand-coloured ribbon-weed hung round his neck like a cravat.

The boat was now leaning at such an angle that Jeremy had difficulty in reaching the wheelhouse. The mist swirled thickly even in there. Bilge-water slapped about his ankles. His feet found little purchase on the tilted deck. Slithering, scrambling, sliding, Jeremy advanced until his hand closed about a heavy spanner. With a sigh of relief, he backed clumsily out.

The Captain was lying halfway over the gunwale, his concrete casing not yet heaved aboard. His shoulders shook with the effort. Jeremy lifted the spanner. Never had he imagined he would do such a thing, but he reminded himself that in self-defence anything was permitted. Besides, he was not committing murder: the Captain was already dead.

None the less, the hollow sound of the Captain's skull shattering was the most horrible he had ever heard. No blood flowed from this skeletal figure, but he could see the depression under the dark hair. Where the hair parted he saw fragments of white bone appearing. The Captain neither moved nor made a sound. Indeed, the blow seemed not to have registered, for a moment later he shook himself and heaved again.

Jeremy lost all control. Again and again he brought the spanner down on the Captain, striking any part of him he could reach, until he missed his aim, the spanner struck the concrete with a force that sent pain shooting up Jeremy's forearm, glanced off and fell into the sea.

In the silence he heard the Captain's laboured breathing, saw the shattered fingers take fresh hold, as the dead man gathered himself for a final effort. With a scream, muffled by the mist, Jeremy flung himself against the far side of the launch in an effort to counterbalance with his weight the inert mass of the Captain, whose concrete casing crashed sickeningly against the side.

With a last grunt or grind the Captain heaved himself on deck. The planking splintered. The motor launch was already down by the

stern. Now she heeled over very gently, tipping Jeremy un-
concernedly into the sea. He heard the dull, almost soundless splash
of a heavy body entering water, had a glimpse of his boat floating
bottom up, and then something struck him a great blow and his head
exploded into pain and coloured lights and blackness, and only his
inflated life-jacket kept his body afloat.

Shortly afterwards the fog was dispersed by the land breeze and
Jeremy's body was picked up by a fishing boat returning to port. He
was alive, but unconscious from a skull fracture, and taken to
hospital. The shattered motor launch was towed ashore. That
evening the accident, and what could have caused it with such an
experienced sailor, was the sole topic of conversation in the
Smugglers' Rest.

But Jeremy's fate was soon blown literally from the minds of the
bar-room frequenters by an even more phenomenal event. The land
breeze freshened steadily and strongly until it reached gale force. It
blew itself out overnight, but it was one of the worst summer squalls
South Cornwall could remember. From every port came news of
damage and narrow escapes. When it became known that a pleasure
vessel, with fourteen aboard including children, had not made it safe
to port, the tragedy overshadowed the accident to Jeremy Sparrow,
who was in any case off the danger list. And as the gale subsided,
Nancarrow had something else to talk of, for the Captain had
disappeared.

Where his place had been between the rocks, a gap had opened.
He who for seventy years had withstood the pounding of the seas had
fallen victim at last to the savagery of a summer gale and disappeared forever, to rest on the bottom of the sea.

"He'll be happier so," was the general verdict. "But who'd have
thought he'd go like that!"

It was Ned Jarvis who told Jeremy what had happened to the
Captain. To his astonishment, the young man shuddered and said,
"I know."

He was still weak, but deemed fit enough for brief visits. Ned began to wonder if this were correct.

"Who told you?" he demanded.

"Nobody. I saw him. It was the Captain who sank my boat."

No one had warned Ned that Jeremy's mind was affected. The old sailor moved his chair a little farther from the bed.

"The old devil!" he murmured soothingly.

"You don't believe me, do you?" Jeremy said.

Ned tried to be diplomatic. "You've had a nasty bang on the head."

"But I can remember what happened to me. I saw the *Ottawa.*"

Like most sailors, Ned was superstitious. He had heard of ghosts at sea. He listened respectfully to Jeremy's story. "I suppose it's possible," he said.

But the Captain was something different. He was no ghost but a solid concrete block. Of course young Jeremy had been disrespectful towards him, but the story was a tall one, even so.

Jeremy shifted impatiently. "How do you suppose my boat got stove in? There were no rocks in the bay where I was drifting. And if there had been, she'd have been holed keel first, not through her deck."

The mysterious damage to the boat had been one of the Smugglers' Rest's chief topics. "It's as if something fell on her," someone had said. Ned Jarvis came to a sudden decision.

"You may be right. I'm not saying it ain't possible. But if I were you I'd keep all this to yourself."

Jeremy began to protest. He had been going to make a story of it, and a journalist's silence was not to be bought.

"Talk all you like," Ned said, "but no one'll believe you. They'll say you've been knocked silly, that's all."

"But it's a fact!"

"And how do you think you're going to prove it? Folks in Nan-carrow won't help. We're only too glad to be rid of the Captain. We want him to rest in peace."

Jeremy saw the force of Ned's arguments. He could imagine what his editor would say if he ever tried to put over such a story. Perhaps silence, after all, was best.

So Jeremy Sparrow returned to London, unaware—like guests at the Smugglers' Rest—that the story had a sting in the tail. An oak plank, in surprisingly good condition and bearing the name *Ottawa*, had been washed up on a lonely beach. The man who found it was a local. He went to the coastguard, another local man. No vessel bearing that name had been reported lost or missing since the brig of seventy years before. The men of Nancarrow took council, their closed fishermen's community reasserting itself, and the plank was laid to rest in the churchyard of Nancarrow, near the graves of the *Ottawa*'s crew.

THE SIN-EATER

ALTHOUGH THE REFORMATION DESTROYED MOST OF THE ROOD-LOFTS that formerly dignified English parish churches, one or two have survived in out-of-the-way places sufficiently inaccessible to discourage even Puritan zeal: remote Devon fastnesses, or villages and the remains of villages along the Welsh Border, before the real mountains start. One of the best preserved is at Penrhayader, well worth a visit for those who do not mind narrow roads, sharp bends, steep gradients, a trek through the mud of a farmyard, and an abrupt climb to the church. Clive Tomlinson was one who counted these deterrents an attraction. On an October day he arrived at the churchyard gate.

It is not necessary to observe that Clive was interested in old churches. No one came to Penrhayader who was not. It had been a village and was now something less than a hamlet, and what was left of it was half a mile away. In the fourteenth century it had no doubt clustered round the church mound; by the twentieth it had receded — perhaps symbolically. Only the farm, whose stonework looked as old as the church's, remained out of apathy.

Clive, surveying the scene from the churchyard, was not particularly concerned with the how or why. It was typical of his unquestioning, uncomplicated nature, as well-meaning as the printed verse in a Christmas card. Like the card, too, he was a symbol of goodwill towards all men. His life was one perpetual effort to be liked. This had naturally resulted in considerable unpopularity. His late-autumn holiday was being spent alone.

He had hired a small car and set out with no clear idea of where he was going, except that he was heading west. The roads were uncrowded in October; it seemed he could go where he would. Hotels had plenty of accommodation; the whole trip was so easy it was dull. Or perhaps he was bored by shortage of society. In this mood Clive came to Carringford.

Carringford is a county town not a hundred and fifty miles from London, but for all that, decidedly off the map. To the discerning this is its charm, and Clive was intermittently discerning. He surveyed it and decided to stop. The Red Lion was comfortable and quiet, its only other guest as solitary as himself and not disposed to hold long conversations, for he was an archivist at work in the Cathedral Muniment Room.

It was the archivist, Henry Robinson, who alerted Clive to the existence of Penrhayader church, for, finding that the young man was an architectural draughtsman, he mentioned the well-preserved rood-loft. No more was needed to send Clive off on a visit. He excelled at pencil sketches of architectural detail. Someday he intended to compile a book on *English Church Interiors in the Middle Ages.* Meanwhile he sketched diligently the unusual and the quaint.

Although it was October, the day was as warm as summer. Late bees were buzzing in the hedges, where blackberries glistened and sloes waited to sweeten in the frost. Clive had passed through cider orchards, skirted magnificent tree-clad hills, noted barns piled with hay for the winter and clamps of turnips, mangolds, and swedes. But as he approached the Welsh Border and its bleak hill-slopes terraced with sheep-runs, the farmer's lot by comparison was poor. When he had picked his way through the farm below the church at Penrhayader, no one had even come curiously to the door. No dog had barked, no cattle had lowed, all was silent; it seemed a house of the dead, especially since the windows were shut tight and curtained, as though the inhabitants were still in bed.

Yet though neglected, the farm was by no means abandoned. A few fowls scratched in the dirt; a pig could be smelt if not inspected; a cat squinted from the window-sill. Only the human inhabitants were missing, and they, perhaps, had merely withdrawn. As he passed, Clive could have sworn he saw a curtain twitch at a window, as though someone upstairs peered out.

Reflecting that country people were often shy of strangers, Clive strode energetically on his way. He was unimaginative and not inclined to introspection. What might have struck another as strange or sinister was to him without significance.

It was after two when he descended from the church mound. The rood-loft was the finest he had seen. A series of sketches reposed in his portfolio. He looked forward to showing them to Mr. Robinson when he got in.

It was as he was picking his way through the farmyard, where the mud and filth and ooze were ankle-deep, that a voice behind him, croaking and sepulchral, enunciated the word "Afternoon."

Clive turned. The door of the farmhouse had opened and an old man stood blinking in the light, like some diurnally awakened creature of darkness, unable to understand why it is not night.

"Good afternoon," Clive responded. His greeting lacked its usual warmth. He had taken quick stock of the farmer, and was not attracted by what he saw.

The old man seemed unaware of it. Clive reflected that country people could be very obtuse. Surely the old man did not suppose he wished to linger in conversation in this unsavoury spot?

The old man, however, appeared to have just that notion. "Fine day," he observed, not looking at the sky.

"Wonderful for October," Clive returned. His voice was breathless as his foot slipped and he skidded in the mud.

The old man stood back and held the door open. "Will you come in a bit?" he enquired.

"It's very good of you, but—no, thank you." Clive felt increasingly the urge to get away.

"'Twouldn't be for long," the old man hastened to assure him. "Just long enough to see my son."

Clive had no desire to extend acquaintance to the next generation. "I'm sorry," he called. "I can't wait."

He made his way across the rest of the farmyard and began fumbling at the gate. It was a heavy five-barred one, fastened by the usual peg and chain. He had opened it easily enough, but now, encumbered by his portfolio and its contents, which he was afraid of dropping in the mud, he found the peg apparently jammed in its chain-link.

The old man watched him from the doorway, but made no move to help. He was short and stocky, with a paunch and a face at once sly and open—shrewd eyes and a toothless idiot mouth. He was dressed in a pair of stained and faded corduroy trousers maintained in place by a belt and a piece of string, and a shirt of indeterminate colour which revealed at the neck an edge of greyish vest. His coat was frayed at the cuffs, its buttons off or hanging, and like his cheeks, his jowls, and his paunch, its pockets sagged.

Clive struggled again with the gate-pin but could not shift it, although nothing held it that he could see. There was no help for it: he would have to climb over, for the old man obviously was not coming to his aid.

He placed one foot on the bottom bar, tucked his portfolio under his arm more securely, and prepared to swing astride, when the mud on his shoes made his foot slip, the portfolio jerked, and two of his best sketches fluttered down. With an exclamation of annoyance Clive turned to retrieve them, but the old man had got there first. He had seized the larger and nearer drawing, and was making off with it towards the house.

"Hi!" Clive called, "where are you going?"

"'Twill dry off better in the house. And you can't put it away all muddy. You'd best come in, I reckon, and dry yourself."

There was some sense in the suggestion. Clive reluctantly followed the old man. His shoes and trouser-bottoms were stiff with mud. Besides he wanted his drawing. If only the place were clean! He had already noted with horror the single tap in the farmyard, the absence of telephone wires, the suspect shack within easy reach of the back door, the cobwebs round the window-frames. The farmhouse, built of stone with a low-pitched slate roof, was unbelievably primitive. Its four small windows barely broke the wall's solid surface; they were not far removed from arrow-slits. Clive could imagine someone holding out in it as in a beleaguered fortress, and the picture did not comfort him. The combination of isolation, neglect, primitive conditions, and his own instinctive repugnance to entering the house or having anything to do with its inhabitants added up to something overwhelmingly grim.

He was unprepared for the heat of the living-room as they entered. Despite the warmth of the day, a fire glowed red in the grate. On top of it a black kettle sputtered. A gridiron leaned against the hearth. All cooking, Clive realized, was done on this fire or in the oven built into the wall beside it. There was no sink, though an enamel bowl stood on the table. Slops and scraps were presumably emptied outside. The ceiling was low and blackened by the smoke from the fire, from candles and a paraffin lamp. The floor was stone, uneven but not unswept, Clive noted. One wall showed patches of damp. In the corner a staircase rose steeply; from the room above came the sound of a shuffling tread. The old man went straight to the foot of the stairs and called softly, "Mother!"

"What is it?" came a voice overhead.

"I've brought a young man to see Eddie."

The voice came to the head of the stairs. "Didn't I tell you someone would be coming? Have faith, Evan Preece, have faith."

"Ay, you were right. You're always right, Becky. Tell me now, are you ready yet?"

"Not far off. Ask the gentleman to sit down a minute. He'll be glad to dry by the fire if his feet are wet."

The old man turned to Clive apologetically, "She'll not be long, but 'tis a woman's business, see. Sit you down until it's time to go up to Eddie."

"I'm afraid," Clive began, "I can't stay."

"You can stay long enough to see my son," the old man insisted. "'Tis the only visitor he'll have. You were sent so that Eddie should lie easy and us have an answer to our prayers."

In spite of himself, Clive found this solicitude for a sick son touching. Within their limits, they obviously gave him every care. And if one were bedridden in this outpost one might go from one year's end to the other without setting eyes on a fresh face. No wonder they were anxious for Eddie to have a visitor; it was an event they would talk about for weeks. It would be churlish to refuse this small act of kindness. Was not one enjoined to visit the sick?

He rescued his drawings from the old man, put them back in his portfolio, and was tying the tapes when a creaking from the corner made him look round; the old woman was coming down the stairs.

She was smaller, frailer, greyer than her husband, her back bowed in what was almost a hump. She wore a crossover print overall on top of her garments, black stockings and bedroom slippers on her feet. She had brown bluish-filmed eyes, moist with rheum or with crying, and she greeted Clive deferentially.

"Would you like to come up, sir?" she invited. "It's all ready for you up there now."

In the background the old man was hurrhing and hawking and trying to catch her eye.

"Did you put the wine out, Becky?" he asked at last in desperation.

The old woman nodded. "With the plate on top of it like you said."

The old man seemed satisfied. "We'd best go up. Lead the way, Becky." He closed in, bringing up the rear. Clive had no option but to pick his way up the steep, narrow staircase which opened directly into the upper room.

The curtains drawn across the small window shrouded everything in a curious daylight gloom, making the low room seem larger and mysterious, although it was ordinary enough. The floor sloped so sharply that a chest of drawers near the window appeared to be tilted on edge, but except for a high-backed upright chair in the corner, most of the space was occupied by an old-fashioned brass-knobbed bed. On the bed a man of indeterminate age was lying, grey-haired but by no means old. His face was sunken, and the deep grooves from nose to chin had not yet smoothed out. His hands were folded and his eyes were closed.

It was so unexpected that Clive, who had never been in the presence of the dead until now, was tempted to turn and run, but the old people were standing as if on guard at the head of the steep stairs. There was nothing for it but to go on as he had begun. Besides, his instinct had been ridiculous. There was nothing to fear from the dead. The still figure—how wasted it was!—could not hurt him. He took a cautious step nearer the bed.

All the time one level of his mind was working frantically in search of something suitable to say. He was not even sure why he had been invited into the death-chamber, nor what response was expected or desired.

"I'm awfully sorry," he said tritely. "It must be very hard to lose a son."

"Ay." The old man nodded in agreement.

The old woman dabbed at her eyes. "Cruel it is, and him not forty." She added inconsequentially, "He was our only one."

The revelation of the dead man's age shook Clive considerably. He had taken him for fifty at least.

"Had he been ill long?" he asked, although he guessed the answer.

"About two year. Ever since they let him come home."

Clive wondered if this meant that the dead man had been of unsound mind as well as consumptive. The parents struck him as being decidedly odd. They seemed to hover, waiting for something. He had obviously failed to find the right remark. Did the old woman expect compliments on her handiwork; "How beautifully you have him laid out"; or the old man seek to have their family resemblance noted, for it was evident that they had been much alike?

His glance strayed towards the aperture in the wall near the bed-head where, quite obviously, there had once been a door. The old man followed his gaze and hastened to offer explanation.

"Couldn't bear to sleep in the back after what had happened, Eddie couldn't. Said he'd rather sleep in the mud of the yard outside." His voice faltered; then he went on more strongly: "So Mother and I had to let him have our room. 'Twas a bit awkward-like, but we'd have done more than that for Eddie. I took the door off its hinges because it squeaked. It opened inwards, you see; it were heavy for Mother to pull it; and we were afraid of waking Eddie with the noise."

"He slept so lightly," the old woman said in amplification. She turned away to wipe the tears from her eyes.

"'One shall be taken,'" Clive observed sententiously in what he hoped was an appropriate tone of voice.

To his consternation, this remark which he had thought quite suitable, appeared to upset the old woman very much. Her eyes filled with tears and her mouth trembled. It seemed that her whole body shook. Her husband laid a broken-nailed hand on her shoulder—a gesture of warning as much as of sympathy—but she shook it off and turned to face Clive in defiance, as though he had insulted her personally.

"Yes, one shall be taken," she cried, "and that the wrong 'un. My son didn't deserve to suffer as he did. I told 'em that, for the wench was nowt but a wanton and there's others to blame as well as him."

"Becky, Becky—" the old man began in protest, but she turned on him. "Hold your tongue, Evan Preece! Why should your own son suffer when there's another more guilty? You know right enough who I mean."

"Ay, I know." The old man sighed heavily. "But 'tis the way of things, Becky, see. That other was—well, who he was," he concluded.

"He's a —"

He raised his hand threateningly. "Shut your mouth!" There was no mistaking his menace. He was suddenly the stronger of the two. The old woman cowered and mumbled, but was careful to keep her words indistinct.

"Now, sir —" the old man turned to Clive as if nothing had happened — "you must take a glass of wine with my son."

For a moment Clive thought he had misheard him, but the old man was already moving to the foot of the bed, where, Clive now noticed, a small table covered with a clean white cloth was standing, and on it a jug and a plate. The plate, posed upon the jug, contained a small round drop-scone, something like a currantless Welsh cake, and no doubt cooked on the gridiron Clive had noticed in the living-room. The jug contained a blackish wine.

As Clive watched, the old man filled a wine-glass. There was only one glass and one plate. Refreshment was to be offered solely to the stranger. It was hardly a sociable meal. And partaken of in the presence of a corpse, too! Clive backed away and violently shook his head. "No, really! Excuse me, but I couldn't. Not — not with your son lying there upon the bed."

"But you *must* drink," the old man exclaimed, "else he'll never lie easy. You must eat and drink to save him from his sins."

"'Tis the last of my blackberry wine," the old woman quaveringly insisted. "I've been saving it for such a day as this."

"Won't you — won't you join me, then?" Clive suggested.

As one, the old people shook their heads.

"Drink and eat," the old man commanded, holding glass and plate outstretched across the corpse. "And may all thy sins be forgiven thee," he added.

The old woman's assent sounded like amen.

Clive sipped the wine and took a mouthful of the round cake. The wine was syrupy and very strong. The cake crumbled to a paste which he forced himself to swallow. It felt as though it were sticking to his tongue. His companions — two living and one dead — were still and silent. Only the old man's breathing sounded loud, and — to Clive —

the movement of his own jaws and the constrictions of his throat as he swallowed, watched all the time by the old woman at the head of the stairs.

Clive had read about wakes and thought they sounded jolly in a macabre way, but this was like no wake he had ever known. It was more like some communion rite. Some mystic rapport between himself and the dead man. His sense of uneasiness increased. He could see no reason to refuse the refreshment offered; besides, he did not wish to offend, but he wished profoundly that he had not been prevailed on to accept it. As he gulped down the last of the wine and the round cake, his gorge rose until he feared he would vomit on the spot. It was as though his stomach itself was rejecting what it had been offered.

He turned to the old woman. "I must go."

Silently she stood aside to allow him passage; silently she followed him down the stairs; silently she watched as he gathered his portfolio together and turned towards the outer door. Then, suddenly, she was on her knees before him, catching at his hand, kissing it with her withered lips. "Thank you for what you've done! A blessing on you for what you've lifted from the soul of my poor boy!"

"Becky!" Her husband's voice sounded angrily as he reached the foot of the stairs behind her. "Let the gentleman alone and none of your carryings-on. 'Tis a miracle that he came, right enough, but we must let him go now — far away from us and our innocent son."

"Yes, innocent!" The old woman's voice rose sharply in a strange, triumphant cry. Her husband opened the outer door and Clive passed through it.

Not one of them attempted a good-bye.

Unfortunately Mr. Robinson was not in to dinner that evening, and Clive, his portfolio beside him, had to nurse his disappointment through three courses and prepare himself for an evening's solitude. He was therefore quite ready to be sociable when Barnabas Elms joined him in the lounge.

Barnabas Elms was well known in Carringford, though it could not be said he was well liked. He was a bachelor, a bore, and a busybody.

Graver charges were hinted at, also beginning with a "b." He was present at many civic occasions in his capacity as a councillor, but was seldom welcome at any of these, partly because he had appointed himself a standing one-man watch committee to ensure that what he called "decent people's feelings" were not outraged. It was Barnabas who rooted out "dirty" books from the Public Library, returning them with the words objected to underlined. It was Barnabas who insisted that shop-window dummies should be discreetly veiled in dust-sheets in the intervals while their clothes were being changed. It was Barnabas who had objected to a nude by a well-known sculptor being erected in the Town Hall Square. Barnabas, in short, who upheld Carringford's reputation for being in the rear of progress and counted this a source of pride.

Having no friends, Barnabas was forced to fall back on the company of his relations, and he had rather few of those. But the wife of the proprietor of the Red Lion was his cousin, and he was in the habit of dropping in. If, as often happened, there were visitors, he would eagerly introduce himself. Since he was a member of the licensing committee, his visitations had to be endured.

Tonight it was Clive's misfortune to endure him. Even Clive found Barnabas difficult to like. He was about to give up trying and withdraw bedwards, when Mr. Robinson arrived. Mr. Robinson had had an excellent dinner with one of the canons in the Close. He had also deciphered a particularly illegible fourteenth-century document and his mood was such that he was prepared to be tolerant of anyone, even of Barnabas, whom he had already met and disliked. Not for a long time had Barnabas been welcomed with so much cordiality. He concluded that here at last was a sympathetic ear, and immediately launched into a denunciation of Carringford's latest offence against decency: the toleration of a coloured family on a council housing estate. Unfortunately—from Barnabas's point of view—there had been no trouble.

"It's scandalous," he complained, despairing of the folly of his fellow citizens. "People will accept anything today. In ten years' time we shan't be able to recognize this city."

"I wonder. Its citizens have some pretty permanent charac- teristics," Mr. Robinson observed. "In the fourteenth century—or so

I have been reading—they confiscated the property of those who traded or visited with the Jews."

"Who's talking about the Jews?" Barnabas demanded.

Mr. Robinson gave a long, exaggerated sigh.

Clive interposed, anxious to smooth things over: "I went to Penrhayader today."

Mr. Robinson immediately looked interested.

"You pick the rummest places," Barnabas objected. "What's at Penrhayader, I'd like to know?"

"A rood-loft in the church." Clive produced his sketches.

"What's a rood-loft?" Barnabas asked.

Clive did his best to explain, while Mr. Robinson examined the drawings, and made gratifyingly appreciative noises, looking up at last to ask, "What's the place like?"

Clive described it as best he could.

"I ask only because I've come across the name in old documents. In the seventeenth century the Puritans classified it as a hotbed of Popery."

"I'm not surprised. It is a very remote village. Old customs have undoubtedly lingered on. I experienced an instance of that while I was there this morning."

"I don't know about old customs," Barnabas interrupted, "but there've been some shocking goings-on there in recent times."

Clive was determined not to be denied his story. "As I was passing the farm by the church—it's very isolated," he continued, "an old man came out and insisted I go in to see his son."

"What did his son want with you?" Barnabas demanded.

"Nothing. When I went in I found that he was dead."

"Perhaps they mistook you for the doctor?" Mr. Robinson suggested.

"No—" Clive shook his head—"they simply wanted me to go in and drink their son's health."

"Drink his health!"

"That's what it seemed like. They insisted I must drink a glass of wine and eat a little cake, with this man laid out on the bed before me. It was all I could do to get it down."

"You mean you had to eat and drink in the presence of the corpse?" Mr. Robinson asked, his eyes staring.

"Yes, and very unnerving it was."

"Could you describe what you ate? Did they say anything to you?"

"I had a glass of blackberry wine and a sort of small, flat, currantless Welsh cake."

Mr. Robinson exhaled very softly. "The genuine articles, no less. And the people — what were they like? Did they give any explanation?"

"Not that I remember," Clive said. "They were very old, very frail, I should think illiterate — "

Mr. Robinson nodded.

"They didn't eat or drink themselves," Clive remembered, "but they seemed terribly grateful that I did. The old man said something about making his son lie easy. I had to eat and drink to save him from his sins."

Mr. Robinson folded his hands in a reverent gesture. "To think the practice still continues!" he exclaimed.

"What practice?" Clive asked, uneasy and bewildered.

"The custom of sin-eating for the dead. It is peculiar to the Welsh Border and is symbolized by the taking of bread and wine in the presence of the corpse."

"And what was the point of it?"

"It was believed that the dead man's sins would be transferred to the account of whoever ate and drank in his presence, thus enabling him to sleep till Judgment Day, provided only that the bread and wine were handed across the body."

Clive laughed nervously. "I took on more than I knew. But why didn't the old people eat and drink to ensure the poor fellow slept easy? He was their son, after all."

"Because the sin-eater must be a stranger, preferably someone who comes from far away, so that when he goes he will take the dead man's sins with him, away from the community in which he lived."

"Like the Israelites driving forth the scapegoat."

"Yes, the two ideas may very possibly be linked. What fascinates me is that sin-eating still survives. It was last recorded in the mid-nineteenth century."

"My grandfather knew of it," Barnabas said suddenly. "I've heard him say he was asked to sin-eat for some man in an outlying village, but he knew what he was doing and refused."

"Should I have refused?" Clive asked. "They seemed so anxious."

"Ah—" Barnabas paused dramatically—"anxious is just what those old folk would be."

"Why they more than any others?"

Barnabas did not answer at first. Then: "Their name's Preece, isn't it?"

"I believe it is," Clive replied.

"And their son's name was Edward?"

Clive nodded.

"Then I wouldn't want to be in your shoes."

"Why? Was Edward Preece particularly sinful?"

"He was a murderer," Barnabas said.

A few days later Clive returned to London, having cut short his stay in Carringford. The sin-eating episode had upset him, although he could not quite say why. On the face of it, it seemed absurd to bother about some ancient pagan superstition surviving by a fluke from the past. Sin could not be transferred; it was against the Christian religion. It was also against common sense.

Nevertheless, the thought recurred to him constantly that he now had murder to his account. He was a murderer and no one knew it — a man who went unpunished and unhanged. Not that the original committer of the crime had been hanged either; he had merely been imprisoned for life, or more exactly for twelve years. "Twelve years," Barnabas Elms had exclaimed, "that's all they gave him! Twelve years for murdering his wife!"

Clive was by now familiar with Preece's story, which Barnabas had needed no persuading to tell. It was evidently one which had made a deep impression upon him. He told it unexpectedly well.

Edward Preece had married his childhood sweetheart, a girl from a neighbouring farm. Elsie had been young and very pretty. Barnabas chronicled her charms. Unfortunately life with Edward and his bigoted parents had proved too narrow for the young wife's happiness. Twice in the first year she ran away and sought refuge with her own people, and twice she returned because of Edward's distress. For Edward loved Elsie to distraction; the world would have been too paltry to lay at her feet. "He spoiled her," Barnabas observed, with the subdued satisfaction of one who has successfully prophesied catastrophe. "He made her feel there was nothing too good for her, so naturally she got to thinking she could do no wrong. And when she found a catch like Dick Roper was after her, she didn't bother to resist for long."

Dick Roper was the only son of the local landowner, an arrogant, swaggering young dandy who had already caused his father trouble enough. Most of the trouble was over women — Barnabas gave details — for whom his appetite was vast. He had done his military service as a commando and then enrolled in an agricultural college, but he had been sent down because of some scandal, and his father was now keeping him on a tight rein, making him live at home, work hard at farming, and take his part in running the estate. Bored, sulky, and resentful, Dick met Elsie. When next he stopped to think, it was too late.

Barnabas had been loud in his condemnation of Elsie, but Mr. Robinson enquired: "Don't you think young Roper was more to blame? He seduced her, from what you've told us."

"Mr. Roper — Sir Richard I should say now — is a gentleman."

"But he seduced the wife of one of his own — or his father's — tenants. I don't call that a gentlemanly act."

"Boys will be boys," Barnabas said with an attempt at lightness.

"And girls will be girls, no doubt. What happened? Did Elsie find she was pregnant?"

"What happened was that Edward Preece found out."

"What did he do?" Clive asked, with apprehension.

"Ah, you may well ask that! It seems the husband was like they say — the last to know — and when he heard, he didn't believe it. He resolved to keep a watch, fooled Elsie into thinking he had gone ploughing, and then crept back towards the house. At the trial he claimed he saw a man cross the farmyard, but from that distance could not recognize who he was. Believing he would catch his wife red-handed, he burst in on her — and found her dead."

"It doesn't sound very likely," Clive objected.

"No. The jury threw it out. For Dick Roper testified that he arrived a quarter of an hour later to find Preece with his hands round Elsie's throat. She had been strangled — there were bruises — and Preece was a violent-tempered man. He had cause for anger — Roper admitted it. What more natural than that he went a bit too far? It is easy to sin." Barnabas sounded as if he had just discovered it.

Mr. Robinson turned on him. "Shouldn't that be a challenge, instead of being put forward as an excuse?"

Barnabas said, smiling smugly, "It is not for us to judge."

"And what became of Roper?" Mr. Robinson enquired grimly.

"He went to Australia. He has a sheep farm in New South Wales. Doing well, too. He decided to stay on out there even after his father died." Barnabas shook his head over this dereliction of duty.

"What about the old people?" Clive asked suddenly. "Where were they while Elsie was being killed?"

"They were out. They claimed they knew nothing."

"And the jury accepted that?"

Barnabas shrugged. "Personally, I'm convinced the Preeces knew something. The old woman certainly did. She tried her best to pin the crime on Dick Roper. But she was too partisan — the judge directed the jury to disregard her."

I can understand that, Clive thought. She'd count each breath Eddie drew, the hairs on his head would be numbered, if his heart so much as faltered she would know. He felt again her withered lips against his fingers, the senile trembling of her toothless jaws. She and her husband had continued to live on that farm where their daughter-in-law had been murdered, to sleep in the very room where she had died. "The wench was nowt but a wanton," Mrs. Preece had protested. "My son did not deserve to suffer when there was others as much to blame."

As in some old ballad where emotions are not explicitly stated, her words were remarkable for what they did not say. Elsie had found life narrow and difficult with her in-laws. Twice in that first year of marriage she had rebelled and run away. It was easy to imagine the unforgiving resentment with which her return would be eyed. She had come back in response to Edward's pleadings, but the old people would sooner far that she had died.

And when she took up with Dick Roper — surely her mother-in-law would be the first to know. Was it she who had told Edward that his wife was no longer faithful, hoping thus to deal his love a death-blow?

There was no limit to the speculations one could indulge in. A thousand questions sprang to mind, destined one and all to remain unanswered. Clive wondered if their urgency would ever recede. For whether he liked it or not, he was now a part of this tragic situation: he bore the guilt though he had not done the deed.

This thought accompanied Clive back to London and was with him in daily life — in his work in the architect's office, in crowded tube-trains, in his bed at nights. He did not discuss his guilt for fear of ridicule. The whole story sounded far-fetched. Who had ever heard of sin-eating? And if he had, who would believe it? Clive assured himself repeatedly that nothing had been altered by his consumption of that tainted wine and bread. In vain. Now that he knew the significance of his actions he felt inextricably bound to the dead.

It was some such powerful but ill-formulated notion that led him to return to Carringford. The following autumn found him again at the Red Lion, where Barnabas Elms, who called by what he termed coincidence on Clive's first evening, inspected the young man with an air of mournful anticipation, like an undertaker visiting a sick friend.

"Returning to the scene of the crime?" he enquired archly.

"I don't know. I hadn't thought of it."

Clive was astonished to hear himself lie so fluently. He had thought of nothing but Penrhayader all the way down. It was absurd, of course, and there would be no sequel to his longing — but he wanted to see the place again.

"The old folks are in the churchyard," Barnabas informed him. "Died last winter. There was no sin-eating for *them*. She went first and he followed. You'll be able to poke around the place in peace."

"I have no intention of doing so," Clive said unconvincingly.

Barnabas shook his head and solemnly closed one eye.

The next day brought a perfect autumn morning, laced with spiders' webs and mist and dew. Clive resolved to delay his visit to Penrhayader no longer, and after breakfast he set out. The drive passed without incident, and, off the main road, there was little traffic about. Within an hour he was turning down the lane leading to church and farmyard, so overgrown that it was almost lost. A robin singing cheerfully in the hedgerow fell silent as he approached. A blackberry trail, bent by the passage of some vehicle, freed itself and sprang back viciously. He noticed then that the hedges on either side of the lane were damaged, as though a visitor had only recently passed. Some other enthusiast to see the rood-loft in the church, perhaps, or a possible buyer for the farm.

Despite this, he almost failed to notice the car when he came upon it, so carefully was it concealed, backed out of sight into a gateway where the hedge was a profusion of blackberry and old man's beard. Clive wondered at the choice of parking place since there was open ground near the farm, but decided the driver must be unfamiliar with his surroundings and had stopped at the first suitable spot.

Clive had no wish to encounter the owner, but the farmyard looked empty enough. He had thought it desolate when he first visited it a year ago, but that was nothing to how it looked today. The peg-and-chain fastening on the gate had rusted. Once again he was obliged to climb. The mire underfoot had dried — from disuse rather than drought, he suspected — and it was possible now to see that the farmyard was paved with flags. But the chickens had vanished; the pig could no longer be smelt; and the door of the lean-to shack near the back porch swung open, revealing the earth-closet for what it was.

As Clive came round the side of the farmhouse, he received a further shock. The downstairs windows were broken and boarded; two planks nailed crosswise barred the door. It looked like a travesty of the plague sign; almost he expected to hear the cry, "Bring out your dead!" Instead the silence was absolute; even the upland wind had dropped. The decay around him seemed that of centuries; he could not believe it was the work of a single year—of a twelvemonth, he thought, reckoning back to his last visit; a twelvemonth and a day.

The coincidence shook him for no logical reason. It was absurd to be affected by a ballad-monger's trite phrase. What if it was the length of time for which fairies were said to bewitch a man, the span between burial and first walking of the ghost? No one believed such nonsense in the twentieth century. He continued resolutely on his way.

It was as he was passing the far side of the house on his tour of inspection that something prompted Clive to look round. The single sash-window on this side was neither broken nor boarded, and a man was climbing out. The window was at ground-level and opened into a dairy. As Clive watched, the man dropped lightly to the ground. He was well-dressed, well-built, but rather stocky. His head was bowed to show dark hair thinning on the top but arranged carefully and expensively. Clive could not see his face.

As though aware of being scrutinized, the man looked up suddenly. Clive noted sun-tanned skin and brown eyes regarding him suspiciously, even while the man politely said, "Good afternoon."

Clive returned the greeting, adding, "What are you doing here?"

"Having a look round." The voice was twangy and unpleasing.

"Are you a prospective purchaser?"

The man laughed silently. "Are you an agent?"

Clive disclaimed all agency connections with such conviction that the intruder almost relaxed. He volunteered a little information: he had known the Preeces once, long ago.

"So did I," Clive said automatically.

"But you're not from these parts."

The stranger rapped it out so smartly that Clive was uncertain what to say. "I'm a visitor here," he offered.

"So am I." The stranger seemed satisfied. Abruptly he switched to something else. "This place has gone to rack and ruin. It's changed a lot since the last time I stood here."

"When was that?" Clive asked with curiosity.

"Years ago." The man seemed about to say more, but refrained. Instead he returned to the farm. "I hear the old folks died only last winter. It must have been in a bad state long before then."

"Oh, it was," Clive assured him. "When I saw it last year I thought no one lived here. But of course they were old and their son obviously hadn't been able to do much —"

The stranger interrupted him: "Do you mean to say you knew Eddie Preece?"

Clive hesitated. Should he tell him? "I didn't know him well," he temporized.

"How long did you know him?" the stranger demanded.

"Not long." Clive was carefully vague. He was beginning to resent the examination. What right had this intruder to question him?

The intruder, however, was unaware of Clive's resentment. Indeed, he seemed unaware of Clive. "Then you didn't know him before," he murmured.

Clive asked very deliberately: "Do you mean before he murdered his wife?"

"So you know!" The stranger seemed almost relieved by this discovery, as though he could speak more freely now. Then an instant later: "How do you know?" he asked quickly. "You said you didn't come from these parts."

"It's no secret," Clive responded. "I heard about it when I was down last year."

"A bad business," the stranger commented. "Eddie Preece didn't deserve to suffer like that."

There was so much sorrow in his voice that Clive was moved by it.

This man must have known Preece well—a school friend, perhaps. They must be about the same age, he decided, trying to cast his mind back to the dead man lying on the bed.

"Why are you here?" he asked again.

"I thought it would be—interesting." The man lingered over the word, as though it had some secret significance. "I like to revisit old haunts."

He smiled then, showing all his teeth in a shark's grin, and added: "Though I should have preferred to be alone."

Clive realized that he disliked this arrogant stranger. "When I saw you, you seemed to be breaking in."

"I was, but there's nothing worth the taking."

"Are you telling me the furniture's still there?"

"It has to rot somewhere, and there's no point in taking it away—it might as well stay here. Since Eddie Preece died first, there's no heir."

"Eddie Preece died a year ago yesterday."

"So you know that too! You seem to be very well informed. But I assure you, I didn't come here to steal, if that's what you're thinking. I've touched nothing. Come in and see for yourself."

With one hand the stranger thrust the sash-window upwards and stood back for Clive to go first. Once again, Clive felt himself out-manœuvred. Who was this man to do the honours of the house?

He stood resolutely still. "I'll take your word for it."

"Don't do that." The stranger's laugh had an unpleasant sound.

Clive turned on his heel.

"Stay!" the other man called after him. "I can show you something interesting inside."

Curiosity is a powerful human motive. In Clive it was particularly strong. He hesitated, and the stranger beckoned imperiously. "It's quite safe, if that's what's worrying you, and I promise I shan't keep you long."

Thoughts of hidden treasure or secret cupboards lured Clive, for what else could the house contain? Reluctantly he put one foot over the sill of the dairy window. As he did so, he was seized by a feeling of horror that he could neither combat nor satisfactorily explain.

The dairy was chill and vaultlike. Its window darkened as the stranger clambered in. Instinctively Clive sought to put a distance between them. For some reason this man affected him unpleasantly.

The dairy opened into the kitchen, which was much as Clive remembered it, though hung with cobwebs now and made gloomy by the boarded windows. There were ashes still in the hearth. The place stank of mice and damp and mildew. Their footsteps rang loudly on the stone floor.

In the corner the staircase ascended, steep and narrow, to the room of death above. Clive led the way and the other followed. At the top he stood blocking the escape. Just so had the old couple stood, Clive remembered, and now they, like their son, were dead. There had been no sin-eating for them, Barnabas Elms had told him. He hoped they lay easy, even so.

It was as he stood in the middle of the room with his back to the window that he thought he heard the sound. A board creaked, as boards do in old houses, but there was something more besides. Without knowing exactly how he knew it, Clive became aware that there was someone in the room next door. It seemed impossible. He glanced at his companion to see if he had heard it. The man was standing rigid, a look of terror on his face. His eyes were fixed, the whites suddenly very prominent, on the open space where once had been the bedroom door.

Clive followed his gaze. At first he noticed nothing. From where he stood no one was visible. He was about to move to the head of the stairs to join the stranger, when his eye was caught by something on the floor. It lay, long and black, stretching out from the empty doorway, unnaturally elongated and — Clive could have sworn — unnaturally dark. Though the light was not strong, the outline was unmistakable. It was the shadow of a man, unmoving, stark.

And not only of a man. The man had a companion, whom he was grasping, in fear or anger, by the throat. It was a woman — Clive could see her long hair streaming backwards, and — quite clearly — the outline of her breast. The shadows were as still as if of statues.

Not even the woman's hair stirred. Apart from their elongation caused by the light's angle, no single detail was blurred.

Clive stood still for so long that he wondered if he too had become a statue—until he heard himself gasping for breath. Or was it the stranger who was gasping? Even across the room, Clive could see that his chest heaved. He was clutching the newel-post at the stairhead. From his colour and posture Clive judged he was about to faint. He glanced again at the shadows. They lay exactly as before. Whatever it was in the next room that cast them, he had to see what lay beyond that missing door.

In three quick strides Clive crossed to where the stranger was standing and gripped him firmly by the arm.

"It's all right. Take it easy. There are two of us. Whoever they are, they won't do us any harm."

He was not certain of this; hence his insistence on equal numbers. His companion relaxed slightly as he spoke.

"Did you see them too? Then they *were* there. I thought I was dreaming. But now, thank heaven, they've gone."

Clive looked and found the next-door room devoid of occupants, or at least that part of it which he could see. He looked at the floor, but the long black shadows had vanished.

"We must have been imagining things," he said.

He knew in his heart that he had imagined nothing, but it was all he could think of to say. He hoped that the stranger would seize upon it. Between them, they would chase these shadows away. And Clive, at least, longed for such reassurance, for without it, what was it that had been in the room next door?

To his dismay, however, the stranger did not seize on his explanations. Instead he said: "We imagined nothing. It was Eddie and Elsie in there. He was standing at the foot of the bed and he had his hands round her throat just like I saw them. Do you think I'll ever forget a sight like that?"

Clive said, without surprise, "You're Richard Roper."

The other nodded impatiently. "Hadn't you guessed?"

Clive knew now that he had guessed; that he had known from the moment he saw him that this was the man responsible for Elsie Preece's death; and therefore the man responsible for the sin he, Clive, now carried.

"I thought you were in Australia," he said.

"So I am—was—until a week ago. Then I decided to come home."

"Why?"

"I don't know. It's only for a short visit. I flew in to London last night, hired a car, and drove straight down here. I wanted to see it *that* bad." Roper snapped his fingers like a man clinching an argument. "Funny how things get you, isn't it?"

He stood there, so sure of himself, so debonair and smiling, even though his face was still blanched with fear, that Clive felt himself choke with rage—an unfamiliar sensation, for his temper was normally cool.

Nevertheless, he managed to master it, and replied, "You seem to have got more than you bargained for."

"You're dead right," Roper said.

"Did you see what you actually saw on that day when . . . when. . . ."

"Exactly the same." Roper indicated the stairs behind him. "I came up there. The house was very still. As I crossed the yard, I had heard Elsie crying out and I was frightened. I had thought she was alone in the house." He grinned suddenly. "Everyone will have told you we were lovers. It was what lent lustre to the case. I used to wait till the Preeces were out and then go and see her. Sometimes we'd meet out, but it was difficult for her to get away."

"But they were out that afternoon?"

"Yes, all of them. The old man had gone into town. The old woman was down in the village. Eddie had ploughing to do. I watched them all set off after midday dinner. Eddie was the last to leave. Elsie waved him off from the door—that was our signal. I knew then that the coast was clear for me.

"It takes about a quarter of an hour from the point where I was watching to get to the Preeces' house. As I crossed the yard, I told you I heard Elsie screaming. I wondered then if Eddie had come back. The screams stopped when I was halfway across the farmyard.

There was a trail of mud over the kitchen floor. It looked as though Eddie had returned unexpectedly. I went upstairs two at a time. As I reached the head of the stairs, I turned and saw them. They were like statues, and Eddie had her by the throat. She was half-undressed, and her clothes were slipping off her shoulders. Her long dark hair had come loose and was hanging down. Her head was limp and lolling sideways. Eddie looked like a man in a trance. I don't believe he knew what he'd done to her—I told them that at the trial. I said, 'My God, you've killed her!' and he looked at me and shook his head— slowly, like a bull that's bewildered. Then he let go of her and fell sobbing on the bed."

Clive listened. The story had a horrible coherence. It also had the glibness of one told many times. He could picture Roper, a little drunk, talking to reporters and pub acquaintances. His dislike of the man increased. He also found him slightly sinister, in a well-dressed, snakelike way. Roper's eyes, small, bright, and unblinking, assessed his every reaction with an intentness that Clive found strange.

And yet not strange, for there was something wrong with the story, and Roper watched to see if this time his bluff would be called. But it never had been, and Eddie Preece had been convicted. Why after all these years should his confidence suddenly fail? Was it the apparition of the two figures that had shaken him, and the memories they conjured up? Or was it simply that he was out of practice? He could not have told his tale for many years.

Clive looked away from him towards the bedroom, empty and rotting like everything else in the house. From the stairhead he could see clearly where the two figures must have been standing, against the protruding foot of the bed. But in the old days. . . . He turned to Roper.

"The door," he said suddenly. "The door."

"What door?" Roper's voice was completely neutral.

"The door that's been taken down. It opened inwards—into the bedroom." Clive pointed. "You couldn't have seen them from here."

"I don't know what you're talking about," Roper said shortly. "You can see for yourself: there's no door."

"But there used to be. At the time of the—the murder. It was only recently the old people took it down. Mrs. Preece mentioned it to me when I was here last autumn when Eddie was laid out dead in this room. They took the door down so that it would be easier for her to get to him if he should want anything in the night."

"Very sensible. That door was a devil to open. The latch made such a clack."

"And it screened much of the back room because it opened inwards. You couldn't have seen the foot of the bed."

"Then I must have been further into the room." Roper spoke easily, but his face had again gone white.

"It would make no difference," Clive responded. "You couldn't see them wherever you stood."

"So?"

"So there's something wrong with your story. It can't have happened the way you describe."

Roper's voice grew colder, more menacing. "Are you trying to say that I lied?"

"Yes, I am. For your own good reasons."

"What do you mean by that?"

"I mean—" Clive paused and swallowed—"that you have something ugly to hide."

Roper laughed, and the sound was chilling. "You've got a nerve, I must say. Are you by any chance accusing me of the murder?"

"Preece always maintained that it was you."

"Preece was a bloody liar and a half-wit."

"So I've heard. Invention wouldn't be such a man's strong point."

"You forget—the jury decided he was lying."

"Juries have made mistakes before now."

"I don't know who you are," Roper said with quiet fury, "but by God I mean to find out. You'll retract that statement in public, unless you want to find yourself in court."

"I may well find myself in court—as your accuser. It was you who murdered Elsie Preece."

"Perhaps you'll be good enough to tell me how this crime was accomplished?"

"Quite easily. By manual pressure on the throat. You watched them all leave except Elsie, no doubt in the manner you describe. Then you stole in like a rat slinking into a corn-bin, and made your way up the stairs. Elsie was expecting you—she was half-undressed already, but what happened then I can't guess. Perhaps there was a quarrel and you lost your temper; perhaps she told you she was giving you up. Perhaps, even, she was importunate and demanded money; or she may have tried blackmail—I don't know. Whatever the reason, you put an end to her, though, as you said of Preece, you may not have known what you did. But she was lying dead on the bed when you heard footsteps approaching. There was no escape, so you did the natural thing: you hid."

"A very interesting reconstruction. Please go on with your detective story."

"The intruder, of course, was Eddie Preece. Eddie had been suspicious of you for a long time—ever since his mother alerted him, in fact."

"She always hated Elsie," Roper muttered.

"This time Preece thought he'd catch you in the act. Instead, he found Elsie dead on the bed, half-naked. He caught her to him, just as you describe, and for a moment they stood just as we saw them—or their shadows. Then he flung himself on the bed and cried."

"I congratulate you on your imagination. But you can't prove any of this."

"Perhaps not—though I'm not sure that I agree with you on that point. I'm certainly going to have a damn good try."

"Try if you like, but not all your depositions will bring Eddie back from the grave."

"Apart from justice, I owe it to myself to clear him." Clive did not feel he could explain quite why. But with every word Roper spoke, he felt the sensation of guilt slip from him. Eddie's sins were whiter than snow. And therefore his sin-eater had a lesser load to carry. For the first time in a year Clive felt himself light of heart. He almost laughed aloud as he announced: "I'm going to have this case reopened. I shall go to London to see my lawyers for a start."

"You won't, you know." Roper spoke very softly. "You're going to stay right here."

There was so much menace in his tone that Clive was frightened, although he could see no reason for fear. Roper was stocky and well-muscled, but Clive was heavier. If he rushed Roper he could almost certainly get past him. He took a step forward.

Roper said harshly, "That's enough."

In spite of himself, Clive hesitated.

Roper said, "It's as well for you you did. I'm not a karate-trained ex-commando for nothing. You move, and I'll break your neck."

Clive felt the sweat of fear on his body. It was unbelievable that this should happen to him — to be alone in an empty house with an uncaught murderer who was preparing to murder again.

He made a gesture of protest.

"Are you going to keep still?" Roper asked.

"What are you going to do?" Clive demanded. He could scarcely speak for the chattering of his teeth.

"See you silenced forever," Roper replied brutally. "You don't imagine you're going to walk out of here? I didn't ask you to come poking around in the first place. You've no one but yourself to blame."

"You invited me in," Clive said stupidly.

"Only because you'd seen the car in the lane. I couldn't afford to have it traced that I'd been here. From that moment it was inevitable that you should die."

Clive squared his shoulders. There could be no rescue; no one even knew where he was. He reproached himself for not having told the proprietor of the Red Lion of his destination, or even Barnabas Elms. But it would have made no difference to his present situation. He resolved to put up a fight, and was mentally rehearsing his tactics when something moving on the floor caught his eye. It was a shadow, but not his own shadow. He was standing still as any stone, whereas this shadow was inching forwards, its menacing hands upraised like giant claws. It was advancing with terrible deliberation on Roper, and whatever cast the shadow was emerging from the open bedroom door.

Clive dared not turn his head to look behind him. There was a coldness, a dankness chill as the grave. It grew in intensity as the caster of the shadow came closer, yet no footfall sounded on the floor. So grotesque and distorted was the shadow that it was impossible to tell if its original were equally so, or whether a normal even if not living being cast it. Clive found he was afraid to know.

Instead he gazed straight ahead at Roper, who had gone deathly pale at the sight of what approached. He seemed unable to move, unable to stop staring with eyeballs that bulged from his head. It was almost as though someone were choking him. His mouth opened but he made no sound; his pale face was suffused darkly; he tottered as if about to fall.

Clive was now enveloped in coldness. There was an earthy smell, as of something long underground. And the shadow now reached all the way to the far wall and began to ascend it, blotting out that corner of the room, blotting out the staircase, blotting out Roper, who gave a dreadful gurgling scream. . . .

Clive was never certain if the darkness was because he fainted, although he heard the thunder of Roper's fall as he bumped and clattered down the staircase. The noise seemed as though it would never end. He put his hands to his ears to try to deaden it, but the sound reverberated in his head. By contrast, the silence that followed was absolute; it had the vaultlike quality of a tomb. Roper neither stirred nor spoke when Clive called him. It came home to him that Roper was dead.

The room seemed suddenly brighter and warmer, the overwhelming shadow had gone. Fearfully Clive looked behind him; the back bedroom was as empty as the front. There was nothing that could cast a shadow; the sky outside was cloudless October blue.

Roper must have lost his balance and fallen; no other explanation would do.

Even so, the accident might be difficult to account for; there were no witnesses—not, at least, whom he could call. Clive went downstairs and touched Roper's warm, limp body. He was lying face downwards in a heap. With an effort, Clive turned him over, and gasped as his heart missed a beat. Roper's face was set in a mask of pure terror. There were the marks of manual strangulation on his throat.

Clive straightened up very slowly. In one way it was a logical end. So it was that Eddie Preece's sin-eater was arrested, charged with murder, and in due course tried and condemned.

IN THE MIST

MARY HESKETH ALWAYS SAID THAT THE MIST WAS RESPONSIBLE. How else explain what happened to her and Ralph? Especially since they were the last people in the world such a thing should happen to: solid, down to earth, prosperous, and recently grandparents for the first time.

It was the arrival of this first grandchild that had delayed their holiday, for naturally Mary could not think of leaving until Jane and the baby were safely settled in at home and had been supplied with every warning and comfort a grandmother could offer, notwithstanding Jane's barely concealed preference for Dr. Spock. Then of course there had been a crisis in Ralph's office—a firm of civil engineers in Queen Anne's Gate—and before they could draw breath their son Peter returned from a student holiday in Spain with food poisoning. It was not surprising their own holiday was late.

Still, as Mary said, the great thing was that they were going. A contented, middle-aged couple with a good car, no worries, and a fortnight's freedom, even in October—it was almost like a second honeymoon. She said so in her artless way to several friends and neighbours, whose degree of cynicism varied, but fortunately not their tact. Besides, it was generally agreed that the Heskeths were an asset to their community — a Surrey village which had been taken over almost exclusively by people like themselves, and in which each detached house acted as a buffer for those adjacent against whatever was unacceptable in the world outside.

The Heskeths had driven north because, from London, there are only two directions the long-distance driver can take and Scotland in autumn struck them as a more desirable goal than Devon or Cornwall, which they already knew rather well. They had excused themselves for not going abroad, which in their circle was more or less expected, by pleading a lack of time to plan. In reality, they were ill at ease with food and languages that weren't English, and believed that there were other things in life besides sun-tan.

It had been Ralph's idea to spend a few days in Yorkshire, a county which he knew well although his wife did not. During the war he had served in the RAF and had been stationed at various bases up and down England's eastern shires. He had never gone back (except once, to attend a civil engineering conference in Sheffield): there were too many memories he would rather leave interred. But twenty years had blunted his emotions and whetted his curiosity. He had a longing to revisit the old haunts.

Mary contentedly acquiesced, as she acquiesced in everything. She was a comfortable rather than a demanding wife. Her view of woman's rôle was based on yesterday's conventions, by which indeed she regulated her whole life. These taught her that there were things in a man's life which it was not for a woman, even the most loyal and devoted woman, to share. So she withdrew to a distance when Ralph went into the RAF chapel in Lincoln Cathedral, or stood lost in reverie before the astronomical clock in York.

How handsome he looked, standing rather self-consciously to attention. And how thankful she was that he had been spared, when so many from these bases had not been. She smiled at him complicitly as he emerged. Until now she had not realized how much these moorlands and fenlands were dedicated to the RAF, having spent the war years in the secluded West of England, where both the children had been born. Ralph had not shared his Service life with her even in conversation, and she had not enquired into it, warned by some self-preserving instinct which told her that ignorance might well be bliss. Like every other woman with a serving husband, she had lived in ever-present expectation of widowhood, and had been both thankful and surprised when that fate failed to overtake her; she had always been premonitorily convinced that it would.

As though to emphasize that all such horrors were now behind them, the October weather was perfect — so much so that Mary, for whom this venture into Ralph's past had the attraction of great danger viewed from great safety, was eager for them to stay another day.

"We haven't seen the Yorkshire coast," she urged, "and I should so like to; and it's not as if we're due in Scotland at any particular time."

So they spent a day of uninterrupted sunshine and turquoise sky and tranquil, sparkling sea, and left later than they intended, as dusk was falling, to drive from Whitby to their hotel near Pickering.

The bracken on the moorland plateau still gleamed redly, though whether in its own right or in the reflection of the setting sun it was impossible to say. It was a world of greyness and redness. The grey road lying like a folded ribbon across the red, flat, featureless moor; the red sun a disc against the soft yet solid greyness of distance and the western horizon. It was this greyness that caused Ralph to step on the accelerator and mutter about fog coming up.

The mist enveloped them suddenly in a slight hollow. In an instant it became impossible to see ahead, impossible to see behind or sideways, impossible — or very nearly — to see the grass verges on the road. Ralph slammed on the brakes and the car's crawl added to the eeriness. The unfamiliar whine of the engine was the only sound. It was only eight miles to Pickering and their hotel lay just beyond it, but in fog so dense it seemed unlikely they would even get that far. An unfamiliar bumping warned them that they had left the metalled roadway. Ralph swore and pulled on the wheel. And then, as suddenly, they were in the clear and the fog patch lay like a solid wall behind them, and Ralph swore with the even greater violence of relief.

Mary patted him. "It's all right, darling. It's over."

"Yes, but God knows when we're going to hit the next."

The moorland seemed all at once to have lost its colour. Grey grass and bracken blended with a much nearer sky. All the horizons had contracted. Whichever way they looked it was a blank — a blank with soft, sinister, shifting edges, which without warning closed about them once again.

It was as they came out of this second fog patch that they saw the young man on the road. They saw him first in the yellow glare of the fog lamp, which seemed absurd in what was now relatively fog-free air.

Ralph switched it off and glanced enquiringly at Mary. "Shall we offer this laddie a lift?"

"Yes," Mary said, influenced as much by the fact that he was the height and build of Peter as by considerations of weather and the loneliness of the road.

The young man turned round as he heard the car approaching, but he made no hitch-hiker's sign. They had a glimpse of a white, strained face above the turned-up collar of a sheepskin flying-jacket. Then the RAF-blue legs marched stolidly yet clumsily on. His step had a martial rhythm. They could hear the left-right, left-right as Ralph slowed the car and wound down the window on his side.

"Want a lift?"

A pair of startled eyes regarded him as though a lift were something unheard of. Then suddenly the young man smiled.

He had a dazzling smile. It lit up a face that was unmistakably good-looking, despite being tired and drawn.

"Jolly decent of you, sir."

The voice was rich and pleasing — a good accent, Mary noted as she leaned back to open the door.

The young man climbed in and she took a closer look at him: dark eyes and hair, and lean, slightly aquiline face. Under the flying-jacket he was wearing a zipped-up RAF battle-blouse. There were heavy flying-boots on his feet. This of course explained the clumsiness of his marching. It seemed an extraordinary garb to choose for walking over the North York moors. Mary was curious; but Ralph was already asking the young man where he wanted to go.

"Back home—to the camp if you're going anywhere near it, sir. It's about five miles from here. We shall pass the entrance on the left."

It was touching that he thought of the camp as "home," Mary decided. She asked politely, "Did you miss the bus?"

"You could put it that way." The young man clenched his hands till the knuckles whitened.

"Will you get into trouble for being late?"

"I shouldn't think so. Not in the circumstances. They're more likely to give me a gong."

Ralph laughed. "You mustn't pull my wife's leg—she won't understand you. Try mine instead; I'm ex-RAF, so that's fair."

"Are you really, sir?" The boy looked doubtful. "But I assure you, I wasn't pulling anyone's leg."

"All right, all right," Ralph said hastily. "I see from the outfit that you're air-crew. What's your line?"

"Pilot."

"We ought to get together—I was a navigator. What kind of crate do you fly?"

"All sorts. It's a Wellington at the moment."

"Don't tell me the RAF still use those! They were obsolete when I came out, and that's some time ago, I can tell you."

"On our field we use them a lot."

"Hear that, Mary? All these millions on defence and these boys have to make do with old equipment. Still, I like your loyalty—not letting the RAF down."

"I've let 'em down all right tonight."

"Checking in late isn't all that serious, is it?"

"I ought to have made it. *I ought.*"

Surprised by the intensity in the boy's voice, Mary turned. He was leaning forward, and his clenched fists beat on his knees.

"I'm sure they'll understand," she said soothingly.

"Oh, yes." His voice was bitter. "But the boys who trusted me won't. They can't. They were so sure I could make it. I was sure too. I almost did. And then, just at the end. . . ." A tear glistened on his cheek.

Mary leaned back and placed a hand over the clenched fist, which was cold and rigid. "Don't torture yourself. I'm sure they know you did the best you could."

"I wonder. It would make it easier to think so."

"Weren't you expecting a gong for it?" Ralph asked.

"I just said that because it shows the stupidity of medals. I get it and they've earned it. Is that fair?"

"I used to ask the same sort of questions. Now I know that even to ask them isn't fair, since it puts the burden of replying on one person rather than another."

"I beg your pardon?"

"I wasn't meaning myself. I've nothing to complain of. Life's been pretty good to me. But why me, for Christ's sake? What have I done to deserve a whole skin, a good job, a wife and kids, and now a grandchild?"

"I envy you the wife and kids."

"Plenty of time. You don't want to settle down too early; at least, that's what I tell my son."

Mary turned back to him. "And how old were you when you married? Fifty?"

"You heard me say I was a lucky man."

"And I'm a lucky woman. That makes two of us. And this young man is lucky we gave him a lift."

He was indeed, Mary reflected, for the fog was closing in. There had been no further solid patches on the road, but visibility had decreased sharply. The headlights cut a path like machetes through jungle. The young man eyed them with appreciation. "Wizard car," he observed.

She was a Humber Hawk, and the Heskeths had had her less than a year and were still proud of her. Even so, they were so used to blasé remarks from Peter that the comment caused them surprise.

"She's not bad," Ralph admitted.

"Had her long?"

"Eight months."

"I suppose they had her in stock." The young man sighed enviously. "She's got everything, hasn't she? A reminder of what motoring's all about."

Suspecting flattery, perhaps mockery, Ralph said shortly, "She's not a blueprint, you know."

Mary felt it was time to intervene. "Do you have a car?" she asked their new acquaintance, who smiled and shook his head.

"Not now. I did when I was up at Oxford."

"Oh!" Mary exclaimed. "Were you there?"

"I did a year."

Mary faltered. The boy had evidently been sent down. She had heard Peter mention such tragedies, accepting them phlegmatically in the way of the very young. Whereas she never lost an opportunity to enlarge upon them: the waste, the shame of it, the disappointment to all concerned. And indeed she meant every word of these monitory expostulations, so vividly could she imagine her own feelings if Peter should bring disgrace upon her.

Now she was in the same car with one of these unfortunates, and she did not know what to say. She could imagine so easily what had happened: the wildness carried too far, the bitter consequences, the parental upbraidings, the enlisting in penance or defiance, or both.

She asked with all the tact she could muster: "Are you making the Royal Air Force your career?"

The young man grinned, but without humour. "I dare say it will be," he said.

"And what were you reading at Oxford?"

"History."

"Fancy! Our son is up there now doing that. Ralph, did you hear? This young man read history at Oxford."

"Really? Which college?" Ralph enquired.

Upon being told the name, Mary exclaimed afresh. "Why, that's Peter's college! Tell me, do you know our son? Our name is Hesketh."

The young man pronounced it, considering. "No, but then it's four years since I left."

"Still, you must know some of the same people. Peter's tutor is Bernard Williams. Who was yours?"

"Bernard Williams? Must be a new man. I suppose most of the younger chaps have gone. Mine won't have done because he's got shocking eyesight. His name's Appleby."

The name registered with both the Heskeths.

"Not Sir David?" Ralph asked, awed.

"I don't know about the 'Sir.' His name's David. Don't tell me they've made him a KBE!"

"Yes. I'd no idea it was so recent. I thought he'd been Sir David for years."

"Not in my day he wasn't."

"That just goes to show that time is deceptive. Which reminds me—where's this camp of yours?"

"We're not there yet. You'll see an arrow pointing to the turning."

"You don't think we've missed it in this fog?"

"I'm certain we haven't. I know every inch of this moorland."

"Yet you're not a native of these parts."

"No, but I've a friend who lives locally. We go out walking. She's taught me to know my way around." He stopped, blushing to have betrayed the friend's sex so quickly, then went on: "It's thanks to her I knew which road to take tonight. And it's thanks to you I'm going to make it. I should never have done it alone."

"Oh, surely. We've come no distance. Although I suppose the fog makes it seem farther than it is."

"No, by the time you found me, I'd bought it."

"Had you been wandering for hours?"

"I don't know. My watch packed it in when the kite pranged."

"Good God!" Ralph came sharply to attention. "You don't mean you were forced down in this?" He indicated the grey trails of vapour that moved against the windscreen.

The young man looked at them also. "I couldn't quite make it," he said.

"I suppose you radioed your field?"

"The radio was out of action."

"You mean they don't know where you are?"

"I was over the North Sea when the radio packed it in. They'll probably conclude I'm in the drink."

"Good God!" Ralph said again. "No wonder you're anxious to make it. But you know, this damn fog's getting worse. And I haven't a clue where I am except that I must still be on the road to Pickering because there hasn't been another road to turn off."

"There's one now," Mary said. Through the murk it was dimly apparent that the edges of the road diverged. Ralph stopped abruptly and stalled the engine. The silence was absolute. It did not seem possible they were within a few miles of human habitation, of lights, streets, houses, shops—a town.

"Isn't it deserted!" Mary had said that morning as they drove in sunlight. They knew the meaning of deserted now. On these moors there was nothing, not even sheep, only thin soil and bracken, a road that looped from one horizon to the other, and in the distance the clifflike scars of former subsidence. This morning there had been larks and puffy cloudlets. Now the sky had fallen, enfolding the earth. There were drops of moisture on the bracken fronds and on the windscreen wipers. Everything was static, immobile, as under an enchanter's spell.

"You take the left-hand fork," the young pilot said quietly.

There was so much confidence in his tone that Ralph started the engine and edged the car over without any further ado, although normally his navigator's training led him to query anyone else's directions and some degree of argument ensued.

Mary, impressed by the young man's quiet confidence, turned round again to talk. "I'm sure you're a good pilot. I can sense it. How many medals have you got?"

"They don't give medals to good pilots. They might as well issue them with your kit."

"No, but seriously—you have got a medal, haven't you?"

"I'd rather not discuss it, if you don't mind."

"It's pretty difficult to get gonged, except in wartime," Ralph put in warningly.

Mary switched her line of attack. "Tell me about your girl-friend," she commanded.

"What is there to say about her?"

"What does she look like? Is she tall or short, fat or thin, dark or fair?"

"Something in between all three."

"Are you engaged?"

"Not officially. Her father thinks she's too young. And he doesn't consider an RAF pilot a very secure means of support. You know— here today and gone tomorrow. I must say I see his point of view. I said we'd wait, but I guess I stuck my neck out too far in saying it. I'm not sure if we'll be able to." He added, without changing his tone, "The camp entrance is on the left here, sir. That's it. Well navigated. Bang on."

Ralph pulled up. "I don't see any entrance."

The young man pointed to where a narrow road turned off in the darkness, with the familiar metal Air Force directing arrow: RAF Hillingdale.

"That's not the entrance to an RAF camp," Ralph objected.

"Not the main entrance, no. But it's the nearest and will get me home soonest. It's only a quarter of a mile down the road."

"Then let us drive you there. You're in no fit state to walk it. You look all in."

"The lane's too narrow to turn and you'd have to back. Don't risk it. I'll manage all right from here."

As he spoke, the young man opened the car door. He climbed out and stood, already shadowy, beside Ralph's window. The mist swirled into the car, and the young man's figure seemed to sway with it. Unless he were swaying on his feet.

"Thanks for the lift." He bent down and they had a last glimpse of the handsome aquiline face, grey in the greyness, and the flash of white teeth in the familiar dazzling smile. Then he was gone and they heard his awkward marching, left-right, left-right, fading away along the narrow road to the left.

The hotel where the Heskeths were staying was private, small, and good. By the time they reached it — in clear weather, for the mist had not descended from the moors — dinner was officially over. However, the proprietor himself served them in the dining-room and apologized for the absence of his wife, who was not feeling well and had retired early.

Mary told him of their encounter with the RAF pilot. He smiled and shook his head.

"He was having you on. There's been no plane down. We should have heard about it if there had been. News travels faster in country districts than ever it does in a town."

"It was very convincing," Ralph put in in defence of Mary's story. "Except for one trivial thing. He mentioned he was flying a Wellington. Surely they're not still in use?"

The proprietor snorted. "Might as well have said an Avro-Anson while he was about it. There's not a Wellington left in service. The lad must have been lacking in imagination to come up with a tale like that."

"He was a nice-looking boy," Mary said regretfully.

"Most likely been in some scrape — a lass, perhaps — and overstayed his pass, so he was trying to get back quick."

"Yes, he mentioned a girl — someone local."

"There you are. It's happening all the time."

"He was wearing flying-kit."

"I don't blame him if he had it. These autumn mists on the moors are bitter cold."

"Yes, but flying-kit. . . ."

"Hold on a minute. Do you mean a sheepskin jacket?"

"Yes, and boots. . . ."

"You can buy 'em locally. There's a Government store. What's to stop his girl-friend's father or brother owning one and fitting him out when the fog came down? Specially if he'd got to walk back to camp in it because he'd missed the bus."

"You asked him if he'd missed the bus," Ralph reminded Mary.

"So I did. Now what did he say in reply?"

"'You could put it that way,'" Ralph prompted. "Meaning, I suppose, that he hadn't even tried for the bus. No doubt he was otherwise occupied. Didn't he say the wedding couldn't wait?"

"He said he wasn't sure if they could wait for the wedding."

"Comes to the same, I dare say."

The proprietor laughed. "It wouldn't be the first shot-gun wedding round here with an RAF bridegroom. Folks don't even raise their eyebrows at 'em now."

Mary pursed her lips, thinking of Peter.

"I think he'd been in trouble before. It sounded as though he'd been sent down from Oxford. He was at the same college as our son. I must ask Peter if he knows anything about him."

"How will you do that when you don't even know his name?"

"We don't, do we? We told him our name, but he didn't give his in exchange."

"If he was hoping to sneak into camp unnoticed, he wouldn't," the proprietor said firmly.

Ralph laughed. "He was certainly hoping to do that. You never saw such a god-forsaken back way as he selected. You wouldn't have known there was a camp within miles."

"Where was it?" the proprietor asked.

"Hillingdon—no, that's Middlesex. RAF Hillingdale."

"He was certainly having you on." The proprietor chuckled. "Hillingdale hasn't been operational since the war. It's just a supply dump for some of the other establishments, staffed mainly by civilian clerks. I shouldn't have thought they were strict enough on passes for the lad to worry. Perhaps that was one more of his tales."

"But why should he lie so?"

"A taste for glamour."

Ralph slowly nodded his head.

"Some of the wartime atmosphere still hangs around these bases," the proprietor continued. "The lad wouldn't be the first to feel that."

"My husband feels it," Mary informed him. "He was in the RAF during the war."

"Ah, then you'll understand what I mean, sir. These youngsters, they don't know what it was like. They see the glamour, but not what went with it. Some of 'em like to play at how they think it was. And if this boy was educated and imaginative. . . ."

"He certainly carried it pretty far—slipping in by the back gate." Ralph's voice held the truculence of the deceived. "He went up a narrow lane that turned off a few miles before we got to Pickering. Serve him right if he gets ten days' CB."

"Quite a study in deception," the proprietor said thoughtfully. "He must have mugged it all up and no mistake. Twenty-five years ago there *was* an entrance to Hillingdale up that lane, but it's been closed for God knows how long. Well, let's hope he'd taken the trouble to find that out. There's a brick wall across the old entrance and a few thicknesses of barbed wire on top."

"You don't say!"

"Ask my wife about it in the morning. She used to live up that lane. Some of the lads did try to use it as a back entrance—she helped one or two of 'em, I believe. From her dad's garden it was possible to climb the camp fence without being spotted—if you were lucky, and if Nora's dad would lend you the steps."

He paused to chuckle reminiscently. "Some rare tales Nora's got. You'll have to ask her about them—only, as I say, she's not too well at present. I'd appreciate it if you'd let it wait another day."

"You don't look too well, either, Mary," Ralph said concernedly. "Are you sure you're feeling all right?"

"There's nothing wrong with me, darling. It was just—something I thought of."

"But you've gone as white as a ghost."

"That's what I thought of." Mary sounded tearful. "Ralph, I think that RAF boy was a ghost."

"Nonsense, darling. There aren't any ghosts."

"Oh, I know we don't believe in them. But that doesn't mean they're not there."

"Mary! I've never heard you talk like this since I've known you. You must have caught a chill on the moors."

"No, Ralph. I'm all right. It's nothing physical. Only—don't you see?—it's all so frighteningly *odd.* "

"You're telling me it's odd! What's the matter with you?"

"Well"—Mary glanced at the proprietor who had also gone rather white—"you said the wartime atmosphere still lingers. Why shouldn't it crystallize in the form of one of the young pilots?"

"But that boy wasn't a ghost." Ralph had a distinct impression as he spoke of the way the car springs had sagged as the boy had entered it. He had been at least ten stone of flesh and blood. No transparent, luminous nonsense about that one. His footsteps, too, had sounded on the road.

"What are you getting at?" His voice was gentler. Mary, poor girl, was looking decidedly ill. "Do you think he's one of the ones who didn't come back? Is that it?"

"He told us he didn't make it," Mary said. "And he'd let the others down—it was his crew he was thinking of."

"Yes, a Wellington carried five." Ralph hardly realized he had spoken aloud, but Mary seized on it.

"It explains why he said a Wellington, I expect they flew them from Hillingdale during the war."

"They did," the proprietor said warily.

"And it explains why he thought our car was so super. It would be to someone who died in 1945. And if he was at Oxford during the war years, it would have been before Sir David Appleby was knighted. And he only did a year because he was called up—not sent down. Oh, Ralph, I'm *certain* that poor boy was a ghost."

She turned to the proprietor. Her face was flushed now. "Did many planes—Wellingtons—crash on the moors?"

"Ay, one or two."

"Then that proves it. It explains why he wore flying-kit, too. Because that wasn't Government surplus, it was old-fashioned. I realize now why it seemed odd and yet familiar. That was wartime issue. Whether you believe it or not, Ralph, you and I saw a ghost."

Ralph said carefully, "It is—unusual—that all these points seem to add up."

"Not 'seem.' They do. You believe in ghosts, don't you?" She looked at the proprietor.

"I believe it's possible they may exist, though I've not seen one. I believe it's possible it was a ghost you saw. But I believe also that no good comes of speculating about the world after this one. You'd best put it out of your minds. Now I must go and see how my wife is, if you'll excuse me. Good night to you, and I hope you sleep sound. As for the RAF lad, he'll do you no harm, flesh or spirit."

As he turned away, they heard him mutter. "Whichever it is, may he rest easy too."

At a quarter to ten next morning the "ghost" walked into the dining-room.

The Heskeths, who had slept late and were the last of the breakfasters, gazed at him open-mouthed. There was no mistaking him: the same height and build, the same dark aquiline features, although he looked a good deal ruddier by the light of day. He was also dressed in civilian clothes of a contemporary cut and fashion, and walked into the dining-room as if he owned the place.

He passed the Heskeths' table without even an acknowledgment. It was this discourtesy which restored Mary to herself.

"Did you get back to camp safely?" she enquired.

"I beg your pardon?"

The young man looked at her in puzzlement.

"I asked if you got back to camp last night without being caught," Mary repeated.

"I'm sorry. I don't understand you. What camp?"

"Whichever RAF camp you're stationed at. Hillingdale, you said."

"But I'm not in the RAF."

"You were wearing RAF uniform when we gave you a lift about half-past six last night."

"I think there's some mistake," the young man said equably. "At half-past six last night I was in a hotel in Goole."

"But we saw you. We talked to you. You admired our car. You were at Oxford."

"Not me, madam, I'm afraid."

"Wait a bit." Ralph leaned forward. "Have you a younger brother, perhaps?"

"Mum's kept it very dark if I have."

"Or a young cousin?"

"Not that I know of. Why this sudden interest in my relations?"

"It's not nosiness," Ralph explained quickly. "Only my wife and I gave a lift last night to an RAF boy who wanted to get to Hillingdale camp. You're so like him that it doesn't seem possible there's no connection. In fact, we thought you were the boy himself."

"They say everyone's got a double," the young man said, "and you make it sound as if it's true. It couldn't have been me you saw, because although I ought to have arrived for the week-end last night I was caught in the fog and had to give up trying to get here. That's how I came to spend the night in Goole. You can check the hotel register if you don't believe me. I stayed at the Neville Arms."

Ralph looked at Mary. "That seems conclusive. And I must say that, though the resemblance is astounding, the voice isn't quite what I recall."

Ralph did not like to say that the young man before them spoke with a Yorkshire accent, whereas last night's guest had not, but Mary took his point.

"We must have been mistaken," she conceded. "Though I must say it's very odd. I shall keep an eye open for this double of yours, Mr. — er — ?"

"Thorpe, Michael Thorpe."

"Any relation to our proprietor?"

The young man grinned. "Sure. I'm the son of the house."

As though to prove it, he crossed the dining-room and disappeared through the service door.

The Heskeths looked at each other. "What price your ghost now?" Ralph said.

"I still feel I'm right," Mary answered with feminine logic.

Ralph abruptly rose to his feet.

"Where are you going?"

"To look out of the window. I want to see what sort of car young Thorpe has."

A moment later Ralph whistled in admiration. "Come here, Mary. Take a look at this."

Outside was the latest MG sports model, such as Ralph had admired at the Motor Show earlier that year.

"That clinches it," Ralph said. "The owner of that beauty wouldn't have wasted a second glance on our old bus."

"Unless he was pulling our legs."

"But he wasn't, was he?"

"No," Mary said. "It certainly didn't sound like that."

The Heskeths were thoughtful for the rest of the morning. They did not go far afield, contenting themselves with the short drive back to Hillingdale and an investigation of the alleged back way in. As the proprietor had told them, a brick wall closed off the roadway; it was some seven feet high with rusty barbed wire on top. The surrounding vegetation was undisturbed; no one had attempted to scale it. The Heskeths returned even more thoughtful than they had set out.

A hundred yards down the road were two deserted, derelict cottages. Mary drew Ralph's attention to them.

"Didn't Mr. Thorpe say that his wife used to live there?"

"I believe he did. What of that?"

"Let's tell her the story."

"What on earth for?"

"I don't know. She might know something."

"I don't see why she should. Anyway, she's not well."

"She's all right today. I saw her. Walking in the garden with her son."

"We may not see her. She keeps pretty much in the background."

"No matter. We'll tell the story in the first place to her husband, and see what he has to say."

"Michael Thorpe may have told them already."

"I doubt it. He obviously thinks we're off our heads."

"All the more reason for warning his father," Ralph suggested.

"He's not that interested," Mary said.

She was right, as usual. Mr. Thorpe knew nothing when the Heskeths buttonholed him after lunch. To their surprise, he showed signs of such visible agitation that they felt constrained to reassure him at once.

"Of course it wasn't your son," Mary said soothingly. "It's just that they were so very much alike. Except for the voice, they could have been brothers."

"What sort of voice had t'other lad got?"

"Not a Yorkshire voice," Ralph said firmly. "It was rather standard, a good accent. Probably came from the south."

"And otherwise he was like our Michael?"

"As alike as two peas in a pod."

"I don't like it," the proprietor murmured. "If this tale gets round Nora'll be mightily upset."

"We wondered if your wife could throw any light on it," Mary suggested. "You said she used to live near Hillingdale."

"I'd rather my wife didn't hear of it, and I'll thank you to keep mum about this ghost. There's no sense in reopening an old wound."

"What makes you suddenly sure it was a ghost?"

"Because—although I'd not meant to tell you—I know the man you gave a lift to. And he's dead."

"How do you know he's dead?"

"I was the one who found him."

Ralph laid a reassuring hand on Mary's arm. "When was this?"

"Twenty-five years ago."

"You mean—in wartime?"

"Twenty-five years ago last night."

Mary moaned softly. "I was right, Ralph. I knew I was right when he talked about the car."

"I'm not so sure," Ralph said sharply to the proprietor. "Aren't you perhaps covering up for your son?"

"The lad had nowt to do with it. He wasn't even born in those days. I should know, for his birth cost his mother so dear that there've been no more children. You can leave him out of this."

"Then who was the — the person we gave a lift to?"

"A young pilot stationed at Hillingdale. It was a bomber station in wartime — mostly Wellingtons. On the way back from one of his missions, he crashed. God knows how he got that kite across the North Sea. No one ever knew, for the radio packed up halfway. But she was losing height all the time and he had to try a forced landing in fog. Unluckily she dived at the last moment, killing the surviving crew. He was thrown out — alive. He was in pretty bad shape when he recovered consciousness, but he could walk, so he set out to walk across the moors, which he knew — "

"So he told us. His girl-friend — "

"That's right. He'd walked them with a local girl. The irony of it was, in his concussed state he didn't realize his crew had had it. He thought he was bringing help to them. And his determination was such that he damn near made it. He was within a hundred yards of Hillingdale when he collapsed."

"Is that where you found him?"

"Ay. On the road to Nora's cottage and the back way into the camp. There was nothing I could do, but he was a brave man and deserved better. He got a bar to his DFC for that."

"And your son?"

"Nora accepted me soon after, though she'd turned me down twice before. Mike was born the following year, and there's not a better son living, as Nora would tell you if she were here."

"But you don't want us to mention this ghost in your wife's hearing?"

"I've told you, I'd be obliged to you if you'd keep mum. She was very fond of that young pilot. And of course, Mike's his son."

COME AND GET ME

AFTER THE DEATH OF GENERAL DERBY, VC, IN HIS EIGHTY-SIXTH
year the house was put up for sale. The General's wife had died
some years earlier and his son in the war, so there was no one
to inherit. Plas Aderyn was put on the market and found no takers.
No one was entirely surprised.

The house (nineteenth-century) was large by any standards. In
later years most of it had been shut off. It stood in ample wooded
grounds and the woods were encroaching to a point where they
threatened to engulf the house. The banks of rhododendrons bordering the drive had spilled over to create a tunnel of gloom; in
places weeds smothered the gravel; everything was rank and
overgrown. "Needs a fortune spending on the grounds," was the
unanimous verdict. And that was before you got to the house.

"Commanding extensive views over the Elan Valley reservoirs,"
said the estate agent's circular with perfect truth. The view from the
front windows was probably the finest in all Radnorshire. Not for
nothing did the overgrown drive wind uphill. Yet the same chance
that had given Plas Aderyn its spectacular panorama had in a sense

condemned it to death, for the village which had once served its needs and supplied its labour lay drowned at the bottom of the lake. The nearest centre—and that a small one—was now some miles away. The house stood in awesome isolation in a region not thickly populated at best.

So there was good reason for the place to stay on the market, despite a not-too-recent photograph in *Country Life* which gave prospective purchasers no idea of what was meant by "nine miles from Rhayader" in terms of rural solitude. Soon even the estate agent virtually forgot the existence of Plas Aderyn. A winter gale blew his "for sale" notice down. Unless you caught a glimpse of it from the other side of the valley, when it still looked singularly impressive, it might as well have sunk with its village beneath the lake.

It was precisely such a glimpse which brought Lieutenant Michael Hodges and three men to Plas Aderyn on a warm May afternoon. Army units were holding manœuvres in the area whose object was a defence of the dams against an imaginary enemy driving northwards. Hodges, having caught sight of the house and learned in the village that it was empty, had secured permission to set up an observation post in the grounds, the only stipulation being that he should cause no damage. As his commanding officer reminded him, "This isn't the real thing."

Hodges was not an imaginative young man, despite the seriousness with which he played military games. Nevertheless, as his Army Land-Rover turned into the overgrown driveway, he felt a momentary unease. If this were for real, he thought, he would be proceeding with extreme caution, expecting an ambush or booby-trap at every turn. In fact it was more like jungle warfare than an exercise taking place in the Welsh hills. He was almost surprised that the only natives appeared to be birds and squirrels, so unused to man that they were unafraid. The whole wood resounded with birdsong. It was one of the loudest and most tuneful avian concerts that Hodges or any of the others had ever heard.

"You can see why they called it Plas Aderyn, can't you, sir?" said Corporal Miller as they stopped at the foot of the terrace in front of the house.

"No," Hodges said, "I can't. You tell me."

"Plas Aderyn means place of the bird."

"How'd you find that out?" asked one of the privates.

"A little bird told me," Miller said with a wink. It was well known that the Corporal had been out with a local girl the previous evening, so the others did not press the point.

Meanwhile Lieutenant Hodges had quickly reconnoitred and decided to set up his observation post where the Land-Rover had stopped, and where a balustrade, still with a worn urn or two in position, marked the limit of once-cultivated ground. The terrace immediately below the house was slightly higher, but he had ascertained that the view was no better and, as he said, there was less chance of causing damage where they were. He did not specify what damage might result from their presence to a house whose ground-floor windows were already broken and boarded up. Instead, he concentrated on giving orders with unaccustomed officiousness, causing his men to glance at one another in surprise. They could not know that as he neared the house their officer had had an over-whelming desire to run away. If every window had been bristling with machine-guns, he could not have felt a greater reluctance to approach. That there was no reason for this fear had merely made it all the more terrifying. Lieutenant Hodges was not accustomed to nerves. Even now, safely back on the lower terrace, he was uneasy. He busied himself checking positions on a map.

It was Corporal Miller who put into words the anxiety Hodges was suppressing, though the Corporal's voice was cheerful enough as he said brightly, with the air of one intent on making an intelligent observation, "Sir, d'you notice how the birds have stopped?"

Lieutenant Hodges made pretence of listening. So it wasn't his imagination after all. There really was a curious waiting stillness.

He said briskly, "It's probably the time of day."

No one was naturalist enough to contradict him. The two privates were already kneeling with field glasses clamped to their eyes, resting their elbows on the balustrade as they surveyed the road along the lake's farther side. It was as well, since they might otherwise have dropped the glasses when the silence was shattered by a laugh, a terrible, shrill ha-ha-ha that was human but maniac, and seemed to come from everywhere at once.

"It's all right, it's only a woodpecker," Hodges said to the three white faces turned towards him, well knowing it to be a lie.

As if in mockery, the laugh came again, this time from behind them. They swung round as one man.

The house gazed vacantly back at them with a deceptively innocent air. Hodges was reminded of the childhood game of statues. Had it been creeping up on them while their backs were turned? Then he abused himself inwardly for a fool. What had got into him? Could a house move forward of its own free will? Even before the echoes of the laugh had finished bouncing back and forth across the valley, he was striving to get a grip on himself. The echoes, of course, explained the ubiquity of the laughter, but they did not imply more than one man. Some village simpleton, even perhaps a schoolboy, was playing tricks on them.

Drawing his revolver from its holster and wishing that for the manoeuvres they had not been issued only with blanks (not that he wanted to shoot anyone, but it would have been a source of confidence to know that he could), Hodges started to move towards the house, motioning the others to follow him. The distance seemed suddenly vast. His every nerve was tense as he waited for the next burst of laughter. Worse still, he had no idea what he was going to do next. Lead, he thought, I couldn't even lead men to their destruction, though I may be doing exactly that; for with every step he felt the old nameless horror: he did not want to go near the house.

It was Corporal Miller who saved him, by clutching his arm and pointing with a shaking hand, "Look, sir, there's someone at the window. The place is inhabited. There must be some mistake."

Hodges looked and saw he was pointing at a first-floor window directly above the front door. A white blur moved, vanished, reappeared. He ordered one of the privates to take a look through the glasses while the rest of them came to a halt.

"It's a man, sir," the private reported, "a young man with very dark hair. I can't see no more because of the angle and the window being so small. And he keeps ducking out of sight like he was in a punch-and-judy show. I don't think he wants to be seen."

"He's probably trespassing, like us, and doesn't want to be prosecuted," Hodges was saying when the maniac laugh rang out again. This time there was no mistaking its source: the man at the window was laughing his head off, except that no normal being ever laughed like that.

"He's escaped from some loony-bin," Corporal Miller suggested. "He's on the run and holed up here."

It seemed the likeliest explanation. The little group halted uncertainly.

"We'll report it to the police," Hodges said, trying not to let his relief sound evident. "We don't want to get too near. You never know how it might affect a chap as far gone as he is. We don't want him throwing himself down."

The man was leaning so far out that this seemed a distinct possibility.

"Careful!" Hodges shouted. "You'll fall!"

The man looked directly at them for an instant, then waved his arms violently.

"Come and get me!" he shouted. "Come and get me! I'm here. What are you waiting for?"

Suddenly, as though seized by unseen hands, he vanished. The window was nothing but an empty square. The silence was so intense it was as if he had been gagged in mid-sentence, or even mid-syllable.

The men looked at Hodges uneasily. "Well, wha' d'you make of that, sir?" one of them asked.

Hodges said, "I think he's an epileptic. He must have had a fit."

"Perhaps he's got shut in there, sir," Corporal Miller suggested. "D'you think we ought to go and see?"

"Yes," Hodges said, wishing Miller had not made the suggestion. He led the way forward resolutely.

The front door was locked, barred and padlocked, the windows on each side boarded up. The Lieutenant tested them, but everything was nailed securely. There was no obvious means of getting in. Nor was there sign that anyone had tried to. The dead years' mouldering leaves lay undisturbed, blown by past winds into piles along the terrace and rotted down by many seasons' rains.

"Place gives you the creeps, don't it?" someone said. Hodges did not contradict him, but merely ordered, "Let's go round and try the back."

The drive curved round the house to outhouses and stables, presenting the same spectacle of decay. A conservatory, mostly glassless, seemed to offer a means of entrance. Hodges climbed gingerly in. A bird flew out in alarm and in one corner there was a scuttling, but the door leading to the house was locked.

"Perhaps he shinned up a drain-pipe," suggested one of the men who had not yet spoken. He put his hand on one to demonstrate. A rusted iron support clattered down, narrowly missing him, and the pipe leaned outwards from the wall of the house.

"I don't think so," Hodges said quickly. "Let's go back to the front and shout."

They called loud and long, but there was no answer.

Miller suggested, "Perhaps he's dead."

"Dead long ago," Hodges said before he could stop himself.

White faces looked at him. "Cor, sir, d'you mean a ghost?"

"Of course not." Hodges denied it quickly. "Only I don't see how he got in. Unless he got on the roof and broke in that way." He looked speculatively at the trees. There was no immediate overhang, no branch convenient to a window.

"Come on," he said. "One last shout, then we'll go."

The echoes volleyed their voices to and fro across the valley, but the silence remained absolute. Nor was it broken as they returned to the Land-Rover, for no one had a word to say. In silence they piled in. In silence Corporal Miller started the engine, and in silence they drove away.

Lieutenant Hodges did not report the incident, he merely stated that Plas Aderyn had proved unsuitable as an observation post; but during the two days they remained stationed in the district he made some enquiries of his own. The general-store-cum-post-office proved the best source of information because he could go in there alone, whereas in the pub he risked making a fool of himself in front of his brother officers, which he naturally wished to avoid. The news that Hodges had seen a ghost, or even that he thought he had seen one, was not the kind he wanted to get around.

But if ghost it was, it was a recent one, he argued. There had been nothing unusual about the dress, nothing to suggest that the young man was not of their own time, even if not of their world. And Mr. Thomas who kept the general store was very willing to tell the Lieutenant what he knew. Yes, it was seven or eight years or thereabouts since old General Derby had passed on, a fine gentleman he was, and his wife a real lady, he took her death very hardly, and such a pity about his son.

"What about his son?" Hodges asked, his ears pricking.

"He died, sir. During the war."

"Tell me about it," Hodges invited.

Mr. Thomas did not hesitate, merely pausing to serve ice-cream to two small girls and some corn-plasters to a woman with bunions the size of eggs.

"Ever so good they are," he assured Hodges. "We sell a lot of them here. You want to keep some handy yourself, sir, for when you're marching. I first discovered them during the war."

"Of course," Hodges said, "you were in it."

"Three and a half years and for two of them I was overseas. Never came back on leave once in all that time, sir. Quite missed the old place, I did."

"But you came back," Hodges reminded him, "which is more than young Derby did."

"Oh, he wasn't killed in action. He was home on leave when it happened. Drowned he was. In the lake. Accident, they said. Missed his way in the darkness. But you hear so many tales."

"What did you hear?" Hodges persisted.

"Well, sir, I was away, like, when it happened. But some said it was suicide."

"Who did?"

"My dad did, for one. He gave him a lift up from the station—the railway was still operating then—and my dad had had to go down to fetch a delivery. He had the store then, you see. He saw Captain Derby get off the train as if he was sleep-walking and start up the road for home. He had no luggage, and he was in battledress. Looked as if he hadn't shaved for two days. It was a pouring wet July evening—must have been in 'forty-four—so my dad offered him a lift as far as the village and he was glad enough to accept. Not that he had a word to say for himself, just sat there like a sack of potatoes. We heard later he was on leave from Normandy, and my dad reckoned he was dead beat. He had to drop him in the village—there wasn't the petrol to go on, and it's another two miles to Plas Aderyn, but he must have made it all right. Two days later his father reported him missing. Said he couldn't settle and had gone out for a walk at night and never come back. He had the whole village searching, and they found where he'd gone down the bank into the lake. Of course it was hushed up a bit—no one wanted to hurt the old General, and it was bad enough the body never being found. But you can understand why there began to be rumours of suicide. Battle fatigue, I think they said it was. Some officers came down to see the General and it was all very hush-hush—but you know how these things get around. I only heard it from my dad, who had to give evidence at the inquest; he couldn't get over the way the Captain looked that night when he drove him up from the station. Talked about it to the end of his days, he did."

"Didn't anyone else see Captain Derby while he was home on that last leave?"

"Only the people at Plas Aderyn."

"Who was there besides the General and his wife?"

"The General's batman—Taylor, his name was. Oh, and old Olwen, of course. Servants were always hard to come by, with the place being so isolated. During the war they had to shut most of it up."

"Are Taylor and old Olwen still alive?"

"Taylor I couldn't tell you. A few years later he came into money and moved away. Quite a large sum it was, though it was too bad it meant he left his old master. But I dare say the General could no longer afford his pay."

"Why, were they poor?"

"The old man didn't leave anything except the house and some sticks of furniture. There was barely enough to pay the small legacy he left old Olwen."

"Hardly a businessman."

"No, he wasn't," Mr. Thomas said, glancing round his shop and reflecting that he was. "They were well enough off when he came. He had his pension, mind, he wasn't starving, but everyone was very surprised. Didn't leave as much as I shall, I shouldn't wonder." He smiled, self-satisfied.

"What about old Olwen, as you call her?" Hodges persisted.

"Olwen Roberts lives with her daughter now. But she is not good in the upper storey. You will not get anything out of her."

"Is she very old?"

"Past eighty, but she is senile. Go and see for yourself, if you wish. Number two, Gwynfa Villas, just past the chapel. Mrs. Hughes, her daughter is."

When Hodges called on the pretext of being a distant relative of General Derby's, Mrs. Hughes looked at him doubtfully.

"You're very welcome to come in, sir, but Mother's memory's not all it might be. I doubt she'll understand what you want."

Old Olwen sat, a shapeless bundle, her jaws working ceaselessly. She did not look up when they entered, not even when her daughter said, "Mother, there's a gentleman to see you." Instead, Hodges found himself transfixed by the beady black eye of an African grey parrot on a perch beside her. He exclaimed aloud. "You don't see many of those."

"He belonged to the General," Mrs. Hughes explained proudly. "We took him over when the old man died. Couldn't leave you to starve, could we, Polly? A wonderful talker he is, too."

˙Nuts," said the parrot distinctly.

"Not again, you greedy bird."

"Nuts. You're nuts," the parrot insisted.

Mrs. Hughes said proudly, "Isn't he a clever boy?"

"They live to a great age, don't they?" Hodges said. "Is this one old?" He congratulated himself on having avoided a gender, since there seemed some doubt about the parrot's sex.

"The vet says he's fifty," Polly's owner answered.

"Did General Derby have him long?"

"Since just before the war, Mr. Taylor once told me—the General's batman he was."

"Taylor, where are my dress studs?" the parrot demanded in a completely different voice.

"That's the General," Mrs. Hughes whispered as if in the presence of genius. "He imitates all of them—we know what they sounded like."

"Who was the 'nuts'?" Hodges asked, also in a whisper.

"That was Taylor."

"Does he ever imitate General Derby's son?"

"No, because he hardly ever heard him. Captain Derby was away at the war, you see."

"And does he imitate your mother?"

"Oh, yes. It makes me feel quite queer at times. It's her as she used to be. Sometimes I could swear she's recovered, but when I come in it's only Polly here."

"It must be most peculiar," Hodges agreed sympathetically. "Rather like hearing a ghost."

"Yes, there they are dead and gone and that parrot will say, 'Thank you, Olwen, that will do nicely,' just like Mrs. Derby used to say. They were good people, very generous to Mother. It's a shame such a tragedy had to happen to them."

"You mean their son's death?"

"Yes, dreadful to think of him lying at the bottom of the lake."

"You won't fish him out of the lake," old Olwen said suddenly. "He was never in it."

"Now, Mother, you know that's not true."

The small shapeless bundle relapsed into silence. Mrs. Hughes looked at the Lieutenant expressively.

"You see how it is," she whispered.

"You're nuts," the parrot said rudely.

Discomfited, Lieutenant Hodges took his leave.

A year later the unit was back in the Elan Valley for more manœuvres, this time against an imaginary enemy striking southwards. No enemy would have done such a thing, but that merely added to the make-believe atmosphere. This was playing at soldiers on the grand scale. Plas Aderyn was still standing and still empty, but Lieutenant Hodges was relieved to find that he was posted at one of the lower lakes, to hold the road that ran like a dividing line between two levels, where the numbing thunder of the dam, unending, drove everything else out of mind.

So he was not best pleased when someone said to him in the mess that evening, "Hear you saw a ghost up here last year."

Of course he should have known the men would talk and the story get around, yet he was unprepared for it. "I don't know about a ghost," he said shortly. "We encountered some village idiot hanging round an old house."

He gave a brief account of the events at Plas Aderyn, saying nothing about the house being securely locked. "He was getting excited," he concluded, "and I thought it best to come away before we frightened him. You never know what half-wits like that will do."

"Nothing very ghostly about that," the enquirer said in disappointment. "I was expecting a headless lady at the least."

"Where did all this take place?" a quiet voice demanded.

Hodges looked up to meet the gaze of Colonel Anstruther.

Several officers from other units had been invited to observe the manœuvres. Anstruther was one of these. He was a legendary figure, his war service one long record of decorations and citations, and one of the youngest officers to achieve a full colonelcy. It seemed unlikely that his query was motivated by anything other than politeness.

"Plas Aderyn, sir," Hodges said.

"Isn't that General Derby's old home?"

"I believe it is, sir."

"And now you claim it's got a ghost?"

The grey eyes were amused and disbelieving.

"I don't claim anything," Hodges said.

"Very wise. There are so many possible interpretations. The supernatural should always be our last resort."

Hodges agreed with him, though in this case, where he had exhausted all natural explanations, the supernatural was all that remained. Fortunately for him, the talk turned to other channels, and it was only later, after the meal had been cleared away and the company had dispersed for the evening, that Anstruther sought him out.

The Colonel came to the point at once. "Tell me what really happened at Plas Aderyn, Lieutenant," he commanded, drawing up a chair. "I'm sure there's more to it than you told us. Aha, I see from your face that I'm right."

Nothing loath, the Lieutenant went over everything from the beginning. His superior listened without saying a word.

"What do you make of it, sir?" Hodges asked when the silence had prolonged itself into what felt like eternity. "Do you believe in ghosts?"

"I don't know," Colonel Anstruther said slowly, "but if I did I could believe there'd be one here. I used to know the Derbys," he added in explanation. "That was why I was interested, of course."

"Did you know their son, sir?"

The Colonel gave him a sharp glance. "Very well. He and I were at Sandhurst together. Now tell me why you asked."

"Only because I understand there was some question of suicide when he was drowned in the lake while on leave from Normandy, although I understand an open verdict was returned."

"Jack Derby committed suicide all right." The Colonel spoke with absolute conviction. "It was the most sensible thing he could do. He was not on leave; he'd run away from the battlefield. For cowardice in the face of the enemy, he would have been court-martialled and shot."

"Poor devil," Hodges said involuntarily.

"Poor devil indeed. I don't believe Jack Derby was a coward. He'd kept up magnificently until then. It's just that when you're in an exposed position, with no hope of relief or reinforcement and being constantly pounded by the enemy's guns, most of us would walk out if we thought we could get away with it. The trouble was that Jack Derby did. What made it all the worse was that he was the son of a general, and a general who'd won the VC. General Derby wasn't equipped to understand what Jack had been through. It wouldn't surprise me if he hadn't suggested the lake."

"But that would be murder!"

"No more so than putting a man against a wall and pumping lead into him. At least Jack avoided that disgrace, which would certainly have killed his father. But it can't have been an easy decision. On the whole I'm not surprised to hear he's a ghost."

"The old woman who used to work there," Hodges said hesitantly, "maintains he's not in the lake."

"What?"

"Yes, sir. Of course she's senile. I dare say she was getting confused."

Colonel Anstruther showed a trace of excitement. "Where is she? Is she still alive?"

"I don't know, sir. I saw her last year in the village. I can easily find out, if you like."

"Do that," the Colonel said. "I'd like to see her. I'm going to lay Jack Derby's ghost. When a man's dead he has the right to sleep easy. And so have the rest of us."

Old Olwen was still alive. She seemed the same in every detail when the two officers were ushered in, a hunched grey bundle sitting over a coal fire despite the warmth of May.

"Mother feels the cold," Mrs. Hughes explained unnecessarily. "And of course poor Polly does too."

The parrot, who had been dozing on his perch, opened his eyes at their coming. Grey, wrinkled, reptilian eyelids rolled up over his round black eyes.

"Good morning," Colonel Anstruther said cheerily, approaching the old woman with a professional bedside air. "You used to know some friends of mine, the Derbys. I thought you could tell me how they were."

Silence.

"The Derbys at Plas Aderyn," he prompted.

Old Olwen said suddenly, "They're all dead."

"Fancy that now!" Mrs. Hughes exclaimed delightedly. "Mother understood what you said."

Anstruther shot her a warning glance. "Do you remember Jack Derby?" he asked gently.

The old woman's eyes were blank. Behind her, the parrot clawed his way to one end of his perch, then the other.

"Excited he is," Mrs. Hughes informed them. "Come, Polly, be a good boy."

The parrot let out an ear-splitting screech that caused both officers to start nervously.

"Who's he imitating?" Hodges asked.

"No one, sir. That's just his parrot language."

"Sounds pretty bad to me."

"You blackmailing hound," the parrot said distinctly, in what Hodges recognized as General Derby's voice.

Anstruther turned pale. "My God! It's uncanny, I could have sworn the old boy was in this room."

"He often says it, sir," Mrs. Hughes apologized. "No matter who's here. Embarrassing it is."

"You're nuts," the parrot said.

"You're nuts," old Olwen echoed.

Anstruther said, "I should be if I had to live with that."

"That's the General's batman, sir. Taylor," Lieutenant Hodges explained.

"I know. I knew Taylor. But imagine the old General having to live with the fellow everlastingly saying that."

Anstruther drew up a chair and took old Olwen's hand in his strong one. "Tell me about the time Jack Derby died."

The filmed moist eyes rested on his for a moment, then swivelled away, blank.

"It was summer, wasn't it?" Anstruther persisted. "He came home unexpectedly on leave. He went out for a walk one night and didn't come back. They found where he'd fallen into the lake."

Silence.

"Olwen, you may clear away." Mrs. Derby's gracious tones came clearly.

"Yes, madam," Olwen said.

The Colonel tugged gently at her hand. "You remember Jack Derby, don't you—Jack who was drowned in the lake?"

"He came back," she said.

"Yes, I know. He took part in the Normandy landings and then he came back on leave. Tell me what happened, Olwen. I'm perfectly sure you know."

"I used to take his meals. Up all those stairs. I was out of breath, I can tell you."

Mrs. Hughes said, "Fancy her remembering that!"

"You liked him, didn't you?"

"You blackmailing hound," the parrot repeated.

Anstruther looked strained. "Could we move him out?"

"It's your uniforms, sir," Mrs. Hughes said soothingly. "They get him excited, see. He hasn't seen them for years." She turned to Hodges. "You were in civvies when you called last year."

"Quite right. I was. But we can hardly do a quick-change. Should we come back again some other day?" This last was to Anstruther, who said quickly, "Who's to say it wouldn't be exactly the same?"

"The same as before, sir, will do nicely," the parrot said obsequiously. "I wouldn't want anything to happen to Captain Jack."

It gave another ear-splitting screech, and old Olwen said, "It's none of our business, Taylor. I won't go along with you."

"You're nuts."

"Nuts in May," Hodges said, joking. The non-sequiturs were getting him down. He did not feel the same desire as Anstruther to lay Jack Derby's ghost, for time had blurred the terror he had felt as he approached Plas Aderyn. If Jack Derby had yielded to the fear all men feel in the face of danger, he was neither sympathetic nor shocked. It had happened before he was born. In a sense he himself had run away from that laugh—

And suddenly the laugh was all around him, a terrible maniac sound, as the parrot reared up on its perch, wings flapping, while shriek after shriek came from its open beak.

"Come and get me, ha-ha-ha! Come and get me!"

In the sudden silence old Olwen said quite distinctly, "That was Captain Jack."

Colonel Anstruther recovered first. He put a hand on old Olwen's shoulder, almost visibly restraining himself from shaking her.

"What do you mean—that was Captain Jack?" he demanded. Hodges was surprised by the hoarseness of his voice.

The old woman shrank away from him. "I heard him," she said, and began to cry.

"Now you've upset her," Mrs. Hughes said reproachfully. It was impossible to tell whether she was accusing the Colonel or the bird. She pushed past and put her arms around her mother. "There now, dear, it's all right."

"Mrs. Hughes," Hodges interrupted urgently, "do you ever let that bird out?"

"Let him out?" She stared at him stupidly.

"I mean, is he allowed to fly?"

"Oh, no. He mightn't come back, might he?"

"Could he—has he ever escaped?"

"No. We had a special chain put on him. But the General used to let him fly about the house."

"Are you sure he didn't get out?" Lieutenant Hodges persisted. "Just before I came to see you last year?"

If only that could be the explanation! But Mrs. Hughes was

already shaking her head. "We take him outside sometimes in the summer, but we don't let him off his chain."

"No good, Hodges. That would have been too easy an answer." Colonel Anstruther looked suddenly tired. Old Olwen continued to whimper, and the parrot had become a bundle of ragged grey feathers hunched miserably in the middle of his perch. It was as though all three had been diminished by the bird's outburst and could never be the same again. Hodges felt the prickling of goose-flesh. He was unashamedly relieved when the Colonel stood up to go.

Outside, Anstruther hesitated.

"Where to now, sir?" Hodges asked.

"There's no need for you to come," the Colonel said, "but I'm going up to Plas Aderyn. I want to get to the bottom of this."

Hodges's heart sank, but he said dutifully, "I'll come with you."

Anstruther looked at him keenly. "I tell you, there's no need. Jack Derby was a good friend of mine. Besides, I've always felt guilty about him. It was my evidence that convicted him."

"I didn't know it ever came to a court-martial, sir."

"It didn't, but I was responsible for his arrest. Unfortunately, in the confusion he escaped — after all, it was a major battle — and made his way back here. It wasn't too difficult after D-Day; officers were to and fro across the Channel all the time. And by the time the military police got here to arrest him, he was lying at the bottom of the lake."

"Mr. Thomas in the general store mentioned something about some soldiers coming."

"Well, now you know why they came. Naturally, the affair was hushed up in the circumstances. Jack was dead, and there was his father to think of. If it had got out, it would have sent the General round the bend. He was one of the old school: die at your post even if it's pointless, if that's what you've been ordered to do. To use your common sense was to besmirch your honour. I've often wondered if he knew."

"About his son, you mean?"

"Yes. Did Jack tell him? It would have taken some guts if he did. Funny, when you think that Jack was accused of cowardice. Perhaps you understand now why I think the General may have suggested the lake."

"I begin to, sir. The equivalent of presenting his son with a loaded pistol."

"Exactly. Jack may have felt he had good reason to come back and haunt. So I'm going up to Plas Aderyn to see if I can help him."

Hodges said, "I'll come too."

Nothing had changed at Plas Aderyn. It was quintessentially the same. The rhododendrons bordering the driveway might have been fractionally higher; there might have been another slate or two off the roof. One of the urns on the balustrade of the lower terrace had toppled over and lay spilling something more like dust than earth across the flags. As they parked the car a squirrel darted away, chattering shrilly, but no birdsong rang in the woods.

The old uneasiness settled upon Hodges like the weight of a heavy coat. He glanced at Colonel Anstruther, who was looking about him with frank curiosity.

"I expect it's changed since you saw it, sir."

"I never did see it," Anstruther answered. "I wasn't in the habit of visiting Jack's home. It must have been a magnificent place once. Pity it had to go to rack and ruin. Let's go and take a look inside."

Hodges followed, uncertain of how to account for his own reluctance and quite unable to tell Anstruther how he felt. The Colonel was striding boldly forward, as if he were an expected guest. His feet crunched confidently on the gravel. Overconfidently? Were his shoulders too square-set? Hodges dismissed such notions as part of his own disturbed imaginings. After all, he was keeping pace with the Colonel and not exactly hanging back.

By silent consent they ignored the main doorway under its portico and went round to the back of the house.

"Everything's locked, sir," Hodges volunteered. "I tried the doors and windows when I was here last year."

"Then we'll just have to break in, shan't we?" Anstruther said testily. "Most of the glass has gone in the larder window. Help me knock out the rest and see if you can squeeze through."

The Lieutenant was much smaller and lighter than the Colonel; it was common sense that he should go first. Nevertheless, Hodges regretted his lack of bulk and inches. What might be waiting for him when he got inside?

Nothing was, of course, though he heard mice scamper and detected movement in the dust-swathed cobwebs where spiders lurked. He turned to Anstruther. "I'll see if I can unbolt the kitchen door, sir. That would be the best way for you to come in."

The bolts resisted him at first, and when he mastered them they squeaked resentment at their long deprivation of oil. He stepped out to join the Colonel, and as he did so the air was darkened by beating wings. Great black flapping wings that folded and settled about the body of an enormous carrion crow, who perched on an outhouse not half a dozen yards distant and said interrogatively, "Caw?"

"Caw yourself!" Hodges answered in relieved reflex. The crow wouldn't do them any harm. And it was not unfitting that it should preside over what was literally "the place of the bird."

"Ugly brute, isn't he?" said the Colonel. "Bet he's had his share of newborn lambs."

Hodges looked at the cruel heavy beak distastefully. He had momentarily forgotten that, for all its name, the carrion crow did not always wait for death.

"Caw!" the bird said derisively.

"Perhaps, sir," Hodges suggested, "we'd better get inside."

The Colonel led the way through the stone-flagged kitchen towards the hall. Hodges was surprised by the gloom. What with boarded-up or shuttered windows, encroaching trees, and dirt-encrusted panes, very little light entered Plas Aderyn and what there was was grey. There was no trace of the sunlight they had left outside; it was as though the sun had never shone in these high rooms with their elaborate plaster-work ceilings, although the house faced south-west. Nor was Hodges prepared for the smell, a decaying, musty odour that seemed to cling to everything.

"Dry rot here all right," the Colonel observed.

As if in confirmation, his foot went through the tread of the bottom stair. The wood did not snap, it gave way almost with a sigh of protest, enveloping the Colonel's shoe in a cloud of feathery, spore-laden dust.

"Careful, Hodges," the Colonel warned. "Doesn't look as though these stairs will bear us. Keep well away from the centre of these treads."

"Better let me go first, sir," Hodges suggested. "If it bears me, it ought to be all right for you."

He led the way, keeping to the outside edge and walking gently as he gripped the banister-rail. Behind him he could hear the Colonel, who was breathing hard as if short of wind.

The first-floor landing, a replica of the hall beneath it, seemed to have innumerable doors, all now standing open upon the rotting rooms within. Yet Hodges felt himself drawn as if by instinct to the right one — the room above the porch from which he had seen the figure wave. It was a square room, not as big as the master-bedrooms, with dressing-rooms that lay to either side of it. The glass in its sash-window was broken and rain and leaves had flooded in. The mess in the grate suggested that jackdaws had nested in the chimney, and a closer look revealed the body of a bird. Hodges felt the hairs on the back of his neck prickle. He had an overwhelming urge to get out. He glanced nervously behind him as though afraid the door might move suddenly upon its hinges and trap him forevermore. But no. It remained unbudging and wide open and Colonel Anstruther was attentively examining the door.

He looked up as Hodges turned towards him. "The owners of this place didn't intend to be disturbed by nocturnal prowlers. Ever seen such a massive lock on a bedroom door?"

The lock would have done service for a strong-room. It was surprisingly strong, a kind of double mortice which shot two steel bolts into the jamb. The door would have given at the hinges before such a lock would burst.

Anstruther was looking about with interest. "Odd that it's only on this one door." He walked across to one of the master-bedrooms. "The others have normal locks. They must have kept the family jewels in this room. Come on, let's see if they've left any there for us."

Hodges could do nothing but follow the Colonel, but his every nerve cried "Don't!" The square room had an inexplicable atmosphere of terror; all he wanted was to get out. It was as though the walls were closing in on him, the ceiling pressing down from above, the trees massing together outside the windows to prevent any escape by that means. While Anstruther stood still in the middle of the room and stared around him, he walked over to the window and gazed out. He could just glimpse the sunlit terrace like something in another world.

Anstruther joined him. "Must have been lovely once. See what a good view you get of the driveway. No one could sneak up on you unawares. You can see the turn-in from the road and the stretch below the lower terrace. Gave you plenty of time to get the red carpet out."

"You can see the lake too," Hodges said involuntarily.

Anstruther nodded. "So you can. That is, you could if the bars would let you."

"Bars?"

"This window used to be barred."

The Colonel ran his hand down the window-frame which clearly bore the marks of sockets which had once held bars in place.

Hodges shivered. "It must have been like a prison, with that lock on the door as well."

The distress which oppressed him, he realized, was very much like what a prisoner must feel: the caged hopelessness; the resentment of injustice; frustration and self-loathing; envy of all who had the freedom to come and go. He imagined himself sitting at the window, eyes fixed on the empty drive, for in its last years Plas Aderyn could have had few visitors; even a delivery van would have been an event. Then suddenly someone comes, strangers come, a chance of rescue; one leaped up and waved one's arms about: "Here I am. Come and get me. Come and get me!"

"Steady on, old boy," the Colonel said.

Hodges looked down at the restraining hand. Had he really waved his arms and shouted? Was it his own voice he had heard? Or was it the cry of madness or despair recreated by a parrot from the lips of a man long dead?

White-faced, he shook off Anstruther's hand. "My God, sir, this room *was* a prison. It's where they used to keep Captain Jack."

"Jack Derby? Who kept him? What's got into you? You know he was drowned in the lake."

The Colonel's questions came like a hail of bullets, but Hodges was too excited to reply.

"Old Olwen said he didn't drown. She used to bring his meals up. And the parrot heard him often enough."

Anstruther shook him. "Will you kindly explain what you're talking about? You sound beside yourself."

"No." Hodges pointed to the door, where a line of bruised wood showed at shoulder-height. "The poor devil must have beaten his hands to pulp with his hammering. And only his gaolers to hear."

"And who were his gaolers?"

"Why, his parents, Taylor the batman, old Olwen."

Anstruther looked shaken. "I don't know what you mean."

"Let's go outside, sir, if you don't mind."

Anstruther led the way.

On the landing Lieutenant Hodges regained a little of his composure.

"I can't prove it," he began, "but Jack Derby's body was never recovered from the lake and old Olwen swore he wasn't in it. Yet he's never been seen again. So what happened to him when he came home accused of cowardice, with the military police hard on his heels? Obviously death was the neatest solution. But suppose Jack Derby wasn't willing to die? You mentioned that his father would have taken his disgrace hard and might have suggested the lake as an honourable alternative to court-martial. But what if Jack wouldn't agree? The disgrace would become public and the family name be sullied. Sooner than have that, I think his father locked him up."

Anstruther said shakily, "It's possible. General Derby was a determined and autocratic man. But what happened in the end? Where *is* Jack?" He glanced round — nervously, it seemed.

"I think he went mad," Hodges said. "You remember the parrot mimicking Taylor? 'You're nuts,' he kept saying, 'You're nuts.' Shut up here, year in, year out, seeing no one but those four, and with that insistent suggestion — if you weren't mad to start with, you'd probably end up that way."

"It doesn't seem possible," Anstruther said, "that they should keep Jack here in secret for — what is it? Years, you say?"

"He was believed dead and there were only the four of them. Nobody came to the house. Or if they did, well, that window commands a good view of the driveway. Jack could be silenced while visitors were here."

Hodges had a disturbing vision of that wildly waving figure swept from the window as if felled by a sudden blow. Mr. Thomas had described the ex-batman as a big fellow. . . . And no one had seen Jack's corpse.

For corpse there was, Hodges was convinced of it. Jack Derby was no longer alive. He could almost fix the date of his death if he knew when the ex-batman had departed. . . .

He turned to Anstruther. "I'll tell you something else."

Anstruther looked at him in mute enquiry. He seemed suddenly to have shrunk.

"Taylor extorted money from the General as the price of his silence," Hodges said. "You heard what the General called him, over and over again: 'you blackmailing hound.' After Jack's death, Taylor quit with most of the General's fortune. We know he came into money and the General died nearly broke."

"If he's still alive. . . ."

"You could prove nothing. It would be a waste of time to try."

There was a sheen of sweat on Anstruther's face. He said thickly, "Let's get out of here."

Hodges was only too eager to comply. Once again he led the way down the rotten staircase, the Colonel treading at his heels. The isolation, the emptiness, the silence, these were getting on his nerves. It was as if the atmosphere of unhappiness that clung to Plas Aderyn was seeping into his soul.

In the hall a single shaft of sunlight had found its way between the shutter-boards. It pointed like a finger up the staircase in the direction from which they had come.

The Colonel mopped his face. "I don't know about you, Hodges, but I've had enough horrors for one day. I need time to think over what you've said, to get adjusted—"

And then above them they heard the laugh.

There was no mistaking it. Even though the Colonel had only heard it reproduced by the parrot, he knew it at once for what it was. But now it rang out immediately above them, from the empty room at the top of the stairs.

"Come and get me, ha-ha-ha! Come and get me!"

The maniac shrieks went on.

White-faced, Anstruther and Hodges stared at each other; then, with one accord turned for the door.

"Don't go. Come and get me, Anstruther. Why don't you? I'm up here."

The Colonel stopped, transfixed. His eyes sought Hodges. Hodges had also stopped.

"There's someone there," the Colonel whispered.

"There can't be," Hodges said.

They both knew the room was empty. There was nowhere anyone could have hid. If in another room they would have heard him crossing the landing above them. But still the voice went on.

"Come up here, Anstruther. Come and get me."

The Colonel took a step towards the stairs.

"Don't go, sir," Hodges protested.

The Colonel seemed not to have heard.

"That's right," the voice cried, as if its possessor could see them, "since you should be here instead of me."

The Colonel stopped again. His face was ashen. "What do you mean?" he cried.

The voice seemed exultant at being answered. "Don't tell me you've forgotten," it called. "How you turned tail and walked the other way in a battle and I went after you and brought you back. We could have hushed it up, I wouldn't have split on you, but you didn't trust me enough for that. You arranged things, staged some witnesses, and accused me of cowardice."

"Why, you—"

"Liar, is it? All right, come and get me. Come and see what it's like up here, behind locked doors and barred windows where I spent the rest of my youth."

"Jack, I didn't mean—"

"You meant me to be shot. A neat, quick ending, and no risk of my betraying you. When I escaped you were worried, until you heard I'd drowned myself. I wish now I had. My father suggested it, because he thought only of the family name. But I wouldn't agree. I didn't see why I should die when I was innocent. So he condemned me to a living death up here."

"No! It's not true." Anstruther's voice sounded strangled.

"It's as true as I stand here. Come and get me, Anstruther. Come and get me. I've waited for you long enough."

Anstruther was clinging to the newel-post.

"It's no use," the voice went on. "All your honours and your medals can't save you. Your courage was founded on a lie. I know you tried to expiate, but while you expiated I rotted here. Was that right? Was that just? Was that honourable, Anstruther? Is that how an officer and a gentleman behaves? Come up and face me man to man, and see if you recognize me. After all these years I've changed."

Like a man in a dream, Anstruther let go the newel-post, squared his shoulders, and faced the stairs.

"Sir!" Hodges called, not knowing what to say, what to make of these fantastic accusations.

Anstruther took no heed. As if on ceremonial parade, he mounted the staircase, head held high and hand where his sword hilt should have been. Hodges stood watching the stiff back, hearing the steady footsteps, until everything suddenly disappeared in a crash of splintered wood and dust.

He thought he heard Anstruther cry out, he thought he heard Captain Jack's laughter, but he was sure of nothing but the great hole which gaped halfway up the staircase where the rotten timbers had given way.

There was no sound now but a last patter of falling debris. With infinite caution Hodges approached and leaned over, clinging to the banisters, which still seemed firm enough.

Through the dust and the splintered timbers he saw Anstruther lying, his body unnaturally still. But there was something else, something lying beneath him; a glimpse of khaki; a scatter of buttons, tarnished gilt. As the dust subsided, whiteness gleamed. There were fingers. Forearms. Surely that was a skull, still with a lock of dark hair clinging to it. An officer's swagger-stick.

Hodges gazed, faint with horror, fighting against vertigo, to where in the cellars below Plas Aderyn the broken-necked body of Colonel Anstruther lay clasped in the skeleton arms of Captain Jack.

THE ISLAND OF REGRETS

T HE COQ D'OR, A MODEST HOSTELRY WITH AN EXCELLENT CUISINE some twenty-five kilometres east of Quimper, is not crowded in the last week of September; it is too near the end of the year. At the beginning of October the shutters go up for the winter and the proprietor and his wife (who does the cooking) hibernate. The previous week is thus a preparation for this withdrawal; an invisible dust sheet lies everywhere. Not but what they are still exceedingly hospitable — business is business, after all — but only those visitors who think it smart to be out of season brave their welcome, or perhaps a casual traveller passing through.

Peter Quint and his fiancée, Dora Matthews, belonged in both categories. They had deliberately chosen the end of September for their holidays, and they were motoring in Normandy and Brittany. From Dieppe they had come slowly southwards; Lorient had been their farthest south-east call and they were on their way back via Quimper to St. Malo when they stopped at the Coq d'Or.

It had been Peter's idea to holiday in late September and to choose the Atlantic coast of France. Dora, who was still too recently engaged to feel it wise to assert independence, had contentedly acquiesced. It was the first holiday since their engagement had been announced to their surprised small world. They were spending it in getting better acquainted. Such was their relationship.

Their worlds, though surprised, were enthusiastically in favour of their marriage. "Dora," said Peter's friends, "is just the girl for him. Sound, sensible, intelligent, yet not bad-looking—the perfect counter-weight to Peter's intellect and nerves." "In Peter," said Dora's world—that is to say, Dora's mother—"Dora has found a man who needs her love. She can devote herself to him without reservation. It's already obvious how much he owes to her."

Dora's devotion, which had begun before the engagement (and there were some who said that Dora had proposed), was not so much a dreamy-eyed hero-worship as a determination to influence and mould. She recognized—how could she fail to—the superiority of her fiancé's brain, but a position in the Ministry of Agriculture and Fisheries did not seem to her to accord with Peter's worth. Had his opinion been asked, Peter would no doubt have agreed with her, but Dora, beginning as she meant to go on, did not canvass his views on this or any other matter. It would never have occurred to either of them that she might be wrong.

Since coming down from Oxford with a First in Classics, Peter had pursued a decidedly deviating course. A brief acquaintance with the schoolboy recipients of his learning had convinced him (and the staff) that teaching was not for him. An even briefer foray into the management trainee jungle had resulted in an equally rapid retreat. In desperation he sat the Civil Service Examination, and had ended behind a desk in the Ministry of Agriculture and Fisheries. This employment, though not arduous was uncongenial, neither Ag. nor Fish. being much concerned with Higher Things. During the previous winter Peter had suffered a mild nervous breakdown. This was politely credited to overwork.

It was while recovering from it that he had first met Dora Matthews, staying with her widowed mother in the same seaside private hotel. The boarders—no one but the management could have thought of them as residents—were all more or less under Dora's spell. She was young and they, poor dears, were ageing; she was nimbler on her feet than they. This naturally made it difficult to avoid her ministrations; only the spryest and the fiercest got away. The pale young man who appeared among them on Maundy Thursday evening was at once a scapegoat and an answer to prayer. One and all, the boarders conspired to throw the young people together. Never was matchmaking more cooperatively carried out. Not surprisingly, Peter saw a good deal of Dora. Three weeks after he returned to London, their engagement was announced.

Dora was all for hurrying on the wedding, but Peter proved unexpectedly firm. Some instinct of self-preservation warned him that he would be surrendering body and soul. About the body he was not so troubled, being sexually repressed and confused. But the soul—the soul was an entirely different matter; he wanted for a while longer to be able to call it his own.

It was with the intention of deflecting Dora that he had proposed this holiday abroad, alleging that they did not yet know each other as a prospective married couple should. At the back of his mind he half hoped that Dora would raise objections which would enable him to break the engagement off; but as a less naïve man might have expected, she was only too ready to agree. Peter owned a 1961 Ford Zephyr and both he and Dora could drive. A motoring holiday seemed to offer the ideal of leisurely progress and enforced proximity.

Thus they drove one evening from Lorient to Quimper and put up at the Coq d'Or. The weather, which had been bad throughout the holiday, had excelled itself and the rain was streaming down. The equinoctial gales had set in punctually that autumn. Too often the landscape was obscured by trailing clouds and ropes of rain. As for the seascape, it boiled and thundered and spurted, and the spray and sea-mist hung above it like steam.

In the bar, while the proprietor's wife was cooking their dinner, Peter enquired about the sights of Kéroualhac. He was not surprised to learn that they were virtually standard: a savage and magnificent coastline, and a chapel dedicated to some local Breton saint. The proprietor seemed to feel that no apology was needed; it was not for these that people came to Kéroualhac. But he was a good-hearted host and set out to entertain the lady, whose French was so much better than the man's. Peter, struggling to follow a language with which he was not perfectly familiar, was astonished to hear Dora ask:

"What is that island off the coast that you can see from the hill above the village?"

"That, madame, is the Ile des Regrets."

"The Ile des Regrets. Did you hear that, Peter? The place is called the Island of Regrets."

"What are you talking about? What island? I never saw one."

"You were driving, dear. You had your eyes on the road."

"And the weather, monsieur, would have prevented you from seeing it. It is astonishing that it was visible to madame."

"I saw it only for a moment," Dora informed him. "There was a lull in the squall, the mist lifted, and it was there. It looked so near I wanted to put out my hand and touch it. Like a child's toy left floating by the beach."

"The distance is deceptive," the proprietor said darkly, "and the tide-rip has been the death of many a boat. At certain times it is as though all the waters of the Channel were being funnelled through one narrow rocky slit."

"The kind of place one would regret trying to get to," Peter murmured. "No wonder it's called the Island of Regrets."

"No, monsieur, that is not the reason for its title. The island is a magic place. You understand?"

"You mean there are superstitions about it," Dora corrected.

The proprietor frowned. "As you prefer, madame. We Bretons say it is a magic island. It grants the first wish you make when you first set foot there, but grants it in such a way that you will wish it had not been granted. This is why it is called the Island of Regrets."

"How quaint," Dora said. "I do love peasant superstitions. Does anyone live on it?"

"A boat calls once a week," the proprietor said with some ambiguity. "Weather permitting, that is."

"The weather doesn't permit much at present, does it?" Peter said glumly, looking at the lashing rain.

"Courage, monsieur. With us, there is no telling. Yesterday, today, and tomorrow are different days. The weather of one day bears no relation to that of another. Tomorrow may be a beautiful day."

"If it is," Dora said, "I vote we go to the island."

"Impossible, madame. It would be dangerous to go alone, and none of our local boatmen will take you. They say the island is an unlucky place."

"Why? You've only got to make sure your first wish is something innocuous."

"No, the superstition, as you call it, is more complex than that. They say that the island-dwellers—the unseen dwellers—do not wish to have their privacy disturbed. Any violation of their territory is punished. Any theft, however small, will mean your death. Three years ago a boy landed there and ate some blackberries. He died, madame. Here in Kéroualhac he died that very night. You can go and see his gravestone in the churchyard."

Dora smiled. "I'll believe you without that. But don't you think there's a rational explanation? He probably ate poisonous berries by mistake."

"That is what the doctor said, madame. But not a soul in Kéroualhac believes it. Poisonous berries do not look like blackberries. A local lad would not make such a mistake. It is more likely that the island-dwellers were angry at his stealing and punished him according to their law."

"Who are these island-dwellers?" Peter asked curiously.

The proprietor spread his hands and shook his head. "In Brittany, monsieur, we have many legends. We are an old race and I think our forebears are never truly dead. For myself, I prefer not to enquire too closely into the nature of the island-dwellers and I prefer to keep my distance from the Ile des Regrets. If you are wise, monsieur and madame, you will also. And now my wife is calling. Dinner is served."

The proprietor proved a good prophet. The next day was a perfect autumn day. Peter, descending in the morning, found Dora studying a large map in the hall.

"We shall be able to go to the island," she informed him. "There's an excellent landing-place just here." Her finger indicated a point on the north-east tip of the island, where Peter judged the channel to be not more than half a mile wide.

"Is it safe?" he asked uneasily, recalling the proprietor's words about "a narrow, rocky slit."

"Perfectly," Dora assured him. "The tide is on the turn now. By the time we've had breakfast the danger will be over. It's only when the water builds up to a certain level that the funnelling effect is produced. As you see, I've been making some enquiries. There's nothing to worry about."

"I don't want to go," Peter said firmly.

"Nonsense, darling," said Dora, who did. "If you don't believe me, go and talk to the boatmen. It isn't the tide-rip that puts them off."

It was not the tide-rip that put Peter off, either. Dora suspected this.

"Of course," she went on, "if you're superstitious. . . ." Her tone implied that superstition was beneath contempt.

"I just don't see any point in going there," Peter muttered.

"It looks enchanting," Dora contradicted. "If we miss this chance it will certainly be the Island of Regrets."

Peter said no more and they set off after breakfast. He half hoped it might be impossible to hire a boat, but this hope was balanced by the fear that Dora would already have arranged this. He was beginning to know his fiancée pretty well.

Overnight the world had been washed free of impurity; all colours had a clean and shining look. The sky was limpid blue and cloudless, a paler reflection of the colour of the sea. Autumnal tints set off a lingering summer greenness. Around the cliffs the breakers crumbled into foam. The island did indeed look to be within touching distance—a plaything that had been idly cast away.

The houses of the village, narrow and flat-fronted, led down to the jetty and the shore, where the mass of tumbled boulders and rock formations bore witness to the fury of past storms. Trails of ribbon-weed glistened in the sunlight, twined with great branches of bladder-wrack. On the hard several boats were drawn up for inspection and a net was being repaired.

The short cut to the harbour lies through the churchyard, where on the sheltered north and east sides of the grey stone building the dead of Kéroualhac sleep. Plain headstones and occasional crosses give briefly the names and dates of the dead. The grass is scythed every summer; some of the older headstones lean. As Peter and Dora hurried down the pathway, a figure straightened up among the stones. He was standing in the remotest corner of the churchyard, where the herbage was drenched with rain. He had hitched his soutane up above his ankles in an effort to keep it dry, and he held half-concealed behind him a branch of mountain ash with orange berries like beads.

Uncertain whether to speak, Peter hesitated, but Dora was already calling out "Bonjour." The curé came apologetically towards them, picking his way as delicately as a cat. He was wearing socks of stout, inelegant home knitting. Peter noticed that his shoes were down at heel.

"What a wonderful morning," Dora greeted him. She prided herself on being at ease with the Church. "We are going to the Ile des Regrets. Give us your blessing. Your people are all too scared to come."

"You have my blessing, certainly," the curé responded, "but if you are going there, you are clearly not afraid. I wish you a pleasant day and continued good weather." He made as if to turn away.

"Oh," Dora cried, catching sight of the rowanberries, "what a beautiful branch. Is this to decorate the church?"

The curé shuddered and held it further from him. "It would not be suitable," he replied.

"Really?" Dora was politely unbelieving. "It would look so lovely in a vase. Would you like me to arrange it for you? I'm considered rather good at doing flowers."

"You are very kind, madame, but I must not trouble you."

Some memory stirred faintly in Peter's mind. "Mountain ash — isn't that a talisman against evil magic?"

The curé admitted: "There are those who believe it to be so."

Dora, momentarily excluded from the conversation, had not been wasting her time. "There are no mountain ash trees in the church-yard," she cried archly. "*Mon père,* where did you get it from?"

The curé twirled the branch unhappily, "Among the Bretons, the old beliefs die hard. They are faithful children of the Church, madame — never doubt it — but they cling still to certain relics of their past. It can happen that a person dies in such circumstances that these superstitious beliefs come into play. In such cases a talisman may be placed on his tombstone so that his evil spirit shall not walk."

"In the twentieth century!" Dora exclaimed in mock con-sternation.

"We are less advanced than you suppose, madame."

"I never heard of anything so absolutely archaic. Do they really believe that evil spirits walk?"

"Whose grave is it?" Peter asked with growing foreboding.

"A young man, monsieur. You would not know his name. He died three years ago from eating poisonous berries."

"Which he found on the Ile des Regrets?"

The curé looked obstinate and unhappy. "As you say, monsieur, he found them on the Ile. There were those who said he should not be given Christian burial, but with God's help I managed to prevail."

Only just, Peter thought, glancing at the decrepit corner from which the curé had come. "May he rest in peace," he said.

"Amen." The curé crossed himself. "Au revoir, monsieur . . . madame. . . ."

"This place is extraordinary," Dora said before he was out of earshot. "Even the priest is afraid. And the proprietor last night more than half believed what he was saying. I'm so glad we didn't miss this."

Peter's fears about the boat were justified when they reached the harbour; Dora had one already laid on.

"I had to pay the earth," she confessed, "but I know it's going to be worth it. It'll make a wonderful story to tell when we get home."

Peter stowed away the picnic-basket and the camera, which Dora had insisted they should bring. His fiancée irritated him this morning, though there was nothing new in this. Sometimes he even wondered if he would have continued with the engagement if everyone else had not been so sure she was the girl for him. They declared her sensible when she seemed to him merely insensitive. More and more he was reminded that "fools rush in. . . ." But it was not in Peter's nature to struggle hard and long against anything. Dora sensed this, and it had given her the upper hand. They were going to the Island of Regrets because Dora wished it; Peter automatically wished the same.

Their boat had an outboard motor which left a faint blue haze as they put-put-putted away. From the jetty the net-menders watched them, and the gulls screamed in the perennial excitement they display whenever a boat, however small, puts out to sea. Dora was at the tiller (she had claimed to know the channel) and Peter noticed with surprise the way she was hugging the shore. She seemed intent on putting the maximum distance between them and the harbour before setting course for the island in the bay. At last, just before they were out of sight behind a headland, she swung the little boat around, and, opening up the throttle to its limits, made straight for the Ile des Regrets.

At once, angry shouts arose from the shore behind them. Looking back, Peter saw that every man was on his feet. They were gesticulating—beckoning and pointing. One man—the owner?— even shook his fist in the air.

"Are you sure this is the course they gave you?" Peter asked Dora. "They don't seem to like it very much."

"They don't like our going to the island," Dora said calmly. "But we've got too good a start for them to be able to intercept."

"Why didn't they make a fuss when you hired the boat?" Peter queried. "They must have known what you were going to do."

"They may not have asked or they misunderstood when I told them. Besides, I did not let them know we were coming here. I told them I wanted a boat to go around the headland to the next bay."

"You lied to them," Peter said.

"Only because I had to, Peter darling. They wouldn't have hired me the boat if I'd told the truth. In a sense you can say that their own superstition brought it on them."

"The superstition, as you call it, is very real to them."

"More fools they. It's about time they learned to live without it."

"They could no more do that than get by without the air they breathe."

"Unhealthy air," Dora said, breathing it in in lungfuls, while the wind and spray brought colour to her cheeks.

Ahead of them lay the sheltered, smiling inlet which Dora's finger had marked on the map. A wooden jetty, its planking decayed and rotten, was the only intimation that the Ile des Regrets had life. Dora switched off the outboard motor and the engine coughed. It was time to wade through the shallows.

Reluctantly Peter stood up.

"Don't make such a mountain out of it, darling," Dora said sweetly. "You'll have to carry me across the threshold next."

Oh, God, Peter thought, swinging a leg over the side of the boat, which rocked alarmingly, I wish I didn't have to marry this girl.

And immediately his foot touched bottom. He had made his first wish, the wish which would be granted by the Ile des Regrets.

By the time he had waded ashore, carrying Dora, Peter's momentary foreboding had gone. In no circumstances could he imagine that he would regret the engagement's being broken. He might even break it himself. Only—she was the ideal wife for him— everyone said so. Surely so many people could not be wrong? There would be such explanations and recriminations. Any doubt he felt would be dismissed as prenuptial nerves. On the other hand, if the engagement could be broken by Dora or by some force outside his control, he could accept it as the working of fate or fortune, and (after a decent interval) rejoice. The Island of Regrets might be renamed the Isle of Gratitude. He set Dora down on it with a jar.

"What a darling place!" she exclaimed overloudly. "I do wish I could believe in magic, like you."

"I hope that isn't your first wish," Peter said sourly.

Dora favoured him with her most indulgent smile. "Darling Peter, you really believe in it, don't you? Now, stand still. I'm going to take your photograph. You look so sweet, standing there on the edge of the water." She was adjusting the camera as she spoke.

Dora was an excellent photographer. She had an instinctive eye for composition and pose. Peter, normally slight and insignificant, looked a colossus against the empty space of sky and sea. Not that this gave him any satisfaction, as he stood there twisting his face into a smile. He would have given anything to turn and leave the island, but Dora was already summoning him to come on.

In a sense he did not blame her for advancing, for the island looked inviting and serene. From the sandy bay with its high-water mark of shells and pebbles, a track led inland, following the course of a stream. On each side of the bay the cliffs rose sheer and craggy, the ledges occupied by rock-pigeons, gulls, and terns. At the top of the slope where beach and scrub-grass intermingled, someone had built a clumsy cache for the stores which were brought once a week by the boat from the mainland; it was a further sign that not all the dwellers on the island were "unseen."

The path and the stream kept pace along a grass-grown valley. The slope of the land was getting steeper all the way. Looking back, Peter was surprised to see how great was the distance they had covered. The island had the power, it seemed, of suspending time. Then he glanced at his watch and at the sun approaching its zenith; the sense of timelessness was apparent rather than real. They had been walking a good half-hour and he had not noticed, so engrossed was he by the unfolding scene.

Despite the lateness of the season, there were wild flowers in profusion everywhere. From low-growing thickets of gorse and bramble the yellow-hammers were demanding bread-and-no-cheese. The blackberries, Peter noticed, were ripe and luscious; they looked more like clusters of jewels than fruit. It was easy to understand that a local boy might fill his stomach and his pockets. Happily, Dora did not like blackberries. . . . He doubted even if she had noticed their existence; she was so intent on taking photographs.

At the top of the slope the grass gave place to woodland — deciduous trees in shades of autumn gold. On a Breton island trees are hardly to be expected. Peter said as much to Dora, who did not reply. The explanation was perfectly simple, as Peter was very soon able to see, for the centre of the island was a depression like a deep saucer, protected on all sides from the almost ceaseless wind.

The track — path was too grandiose a word to describe it — began once more to descend. In the bottom of the saucer a house hugged a cloak of conifers so tightly around it that only a chimney showed. Perhaps the house would be ruined and desolate, given over to martins and bats. Overhead the pine-trees merged, making the path darker; underfoot the pine-needles carpeted the ground.

"Aren't you glad we came?" Dora called out to him.

This time it was Peter's turn not to reply.

In not-quite-mock anger, Dora pelted him with fir-cones, one of which hit him in the eye. Peter cried out in mingled pain and protest. Dora was instantly at his side.

"Did the nasty little fir-cone hit him, and did his horrid Dora throw it, then! Never mind, Dora will kiss it better." This she proceeded to do. Peter remained unresponsive. She flung away from him in a pet.

"I can't think what's the matter with you this morning. Are you sulking because you didn't want to come? Really, Peter, you behave no better than a baby. For heaven's sake be a sport and come along."

She marched off briskly, leaving Peter to follow, which he did, albeit with resentment in his heart. Neither of them noticed that one of the little fir-cones had lodged in the outside pocket of her bag.

The path through the pines led ever more steeply downwards.

They had left the sunlight behind. The pine-needles underfoot muffled their footsteps. There was something sinister about this absence of sun and sound. Small flies darted about under the pine-trees. A clump of scarlet, white-spotted toadstools made Dora exclaim: "Look, Peter, there's your magic — fairy houses."

"Deadly poisonous," Peter remarked.

The more he penetrated this wood, the more he wanted to get out of it, but Dora boldly led him further in. No wisp of smoke came from the chimneys showing above the tree-tops. The path itself had a little-frequented air.

"Do you suppose anyone lives in the house?" Dora asked him.

"No," Peter said, not wanting to believe.

Almost before they knew it, the house was upon them. A sudden twist in the path and there it stood. Grey stone, foursquare, its windows protected by closed shutters, it had a desolate and unresponsive look. Yet the front door swung open on its hinges; the ubiquitous pine-needles had drifted into the hall. They had also blocked the guttering and the drain-pipes. After the autumn rains damp patches showed on the wall.

All around the trees formed an elliptical clearing, the longer part of which lay directly behind the house. A rusty door-bell, its chain bracketed to the wall to discourage visitors, reverberated when Dora pulled it with unexpected sonority through the house.

"Suppose someone answers?" Peter said with apprehension.

"Nonsense, darling, the place is absolutely dead."

It certainly seemed so; no hesitant footsteps or creaking shutter, no voice sharply demanding "Who's there?" Nevertheless, remembering the cache for foodstuffs and the boat's once-weekly call, Peter's uneasiness mounted. No one had described the island as uninhabited, though they had seen no sign of life between the house and the shore.

Dora, untroubled by these considerations, pushed idly at the swinging front door. It opened inwards with a sudden shrill whine from the hinges, spilling a drift of pine-needles to the floor.

"Why, the place is furnished!" Dora said, startled for the first time out of her phlegmatic calm. "What a shame to let it go to rack and ruin." She was tcha-tcha-ing and inspecting as she spoke.

Peter wondered what the owners would say to two inquisitive foreigners if they found them poking round in their hall; but he was bound to agree with Dora that it was a shame to see objects of beauty and value sinking through neglect into a state of disrepair.

Dora pushed open the door to the drawing-room. It revealed the same melancholy scene. The silk upholstery was split and rotten, the carpet dim under dust. At the windows hung what had once been curtains. Cobwebs trailed and floated on the walls, massing around mirrors and pictures and festooning the chandelier. It might have been the Sleeping Beauty's palace, except that there is nothing fairy-tale about filth.

"The whole place wants burning," Dora stated, sneezing as the dust got into her throat.

"You don't want to go upstairs?" Peter asked her.

She missed the irony of his tone. "I want to get out," she said abruptly. And walked through towards the back door.

This gave on to the long and narrowing garden, whose greatest width was just below the house. It was entirely filled with a rank weed too coarse even to be couch-grass, which had submerged the outline of flower-beds and overrun even the terrace's stones. Unlike the flowers on the island, the weed had faded; its leaves were colourless, deepening to brown. It lay unstirred by the wind within its prison-enclave of pine-trees, for all the world like some malignant, stagnant pond.

And in the middle of it a man was standing, with his head sunk low upon his chest. He stood with his back to the house, and his hands thrust deep in his pockets. His long white beard and hair and old-fashioned garments made him look like Rip van Winkle sleeping on his feet.

"Why doesn't he speak to us?" Dora whispered.

"Perhaps he hasn't heard us," Peter replied. He knew in his heart that this was not the answer, but he obligingly called out, "Good day."

"Bonjour," Dora added for good measure.

The figure neither moved nor spoke.

"He must be deaf," Dora concluded.

"Or dead," Peter added, half to himself.

Dora's literal-mindedness came to her rescue.

"He can't be dead, dear. He's standing up."

"So he is," Peter said. "I hadn't noticed."

She gave him a glance of dislike. "Aren't you going to do anything about him?" she demanded. "Find out who he is or ask him if there's anything he wants."

"*Comment allez-vous?*" Peter dutifully shouted, aware of its incongruous sound.

The man might have been a statue for all the signs he showed of responding.

"Go up to him," Dora said.

"What for? We have nothing we can give him. Remember we're trespassers here."

"Then I'll go," said Dora determinedly. She began to move forward as she spoke.

"Wait," Peter commanded. "You're too sudden. You'll give him too much of a shock."

He began to edge cautiously around the garden. Dora did the same on the far side. Still the old man stood with his head bowed, like a statue. They tried French and English, even German; he did not look up. They were near enough now to see that his clothes were tattered, his hair and beard were matted and unkempt. His face, though grimed with dirt, had a strange, unhealthy pallor—maggot-white, Peter thought to himself. Even Dora's exuberance had subsided. For once she was not taking the lead. Peter stepped forward and laid a reluctant hand on the greasy shoulder.

"Can we do anything to help?" he asked awkwardly. "Is there anything you need?"

At his touch the figure came to life convulsively, broke free of his grasp, and raised its elf-locked head. The eyes, scarlet-rimmed, the lower lids drooping like a bloodhound's, lit up as they contemplated him. The voice was cracked and produced with difficulty, wheezing, as though, like the furniture, it had been neglected to the point of disrepair. His laughter when it came was a shrill cascade of cackles — harsh but not resonant in that oppressive air.

"Come at last, he has, the new tenant," he cried between his peals of hideous mirth. "I could feel it in my bones that you were coming. I've been waiting for you since yesterday."

Peter backed away from the madman. "You're mistaken. I don't live here."

The madman's laugh rose, screeching and unearthly. "Don't try to deny it, my dear sir. This commodious residence is never left un-tenanted. It wouldn't be good for it, you know. I've been wondering who would replace me when I gave up my tenancy, because this winter, I'm afraid I shall really have to go."

He put out a claw with black-rimmed fingernails.

With a cry of fear Peter plunged back towards the path. Dora was already running as if the devils of Hell were behind her, but the madman made no attempt to pursue. He simply went on standing there, and laughing. The sound was audible all the way to the shore.

"The new tenant! The new tenant's coming. They're going to let me give up the keys at last. And the new tenant doesn't think he's going to like it. But he'll get used to it. It's a life-tenancy, ha-ha-ha!"

Peter and Dora were received in Kéroualhac with the same silence that they had preserved almost unbroken in the boat. They were both considerably shaken by their encounter with the madman, but neither was willing to admit as much, Peter because he feared to arouse Dora's derision, Dora because she was bewildered by herself. She was still far from accepting the Bretons' view of the island, but the effect it had on one was certainly very odd. During their flight to the shore she had known sheer unreasoning terror — a phenomenon which had not disturbed her rational mind before. Now, in the sunlight, and with a fresh sea-breeze blowing, she was exceedingly ashamed of this lapse. What was she to say if people asked about the trip to the island? Should she admit her fear, or make light of it, laugh it off? And what would Peter reply if questioned? But there was no need for Peter to speak. His white, set face was an announcement that all had not gone smoothly, even without the nerve twitching in his cheek.

As it happened, Dora need not have worried. No one was anxious to ask. The men on the quayside withdrew when they saw them coming and contented themselves with a long, unfriendly stare. They made no pretence of continuing with their occupations of mending nets or applying a lick of paint. They simply stood there in their uniform seamen's jerseys, dark trousers, and sea-boots, and looked on with a hostile yet pitying air. Even the owner of the boat did not come forward. When Dora approached him, he promptly turned his back. Not even Dora was proof against such a demonstration.

"How stupid they are," she observed as she turned away.

Her remark was audible, but they remained impassive.

"You've annoyed them," Peter said. He longed to dissociate himself entirely from Dora's actions, but this was the most he could do.

"I like that! What have I done that you haven't?"

Peter forbore to explain.

"They're like savages," Dora continued, unabated. "It's as if we had broken a taboo."

"Let's hope they won't turn hostile as savages."

"Darling, this is Europe, for heaven's sake."

"And the twentieth century," Peter added.

Dora saw no connection between the two.

The street from the harbour was silent and deserted. The whole village knew they had been to the Island of Regrets. Children at play were called sharply into the houses; loiterers were seized and cuffed by the maternal hand. Conversations across the street were abruptly ended; the evening rang with the slamming of front doors. Only in the churchyard did the visitors encounter unimpaired indifference, the dead of Kéroualhac having no cause for fear.

"Unfriendly lot," Dora said, referring to the living. "I shan't be sorry to get back to our hotel."

"If it still is our hotel," Peter muttered.

Dora looked at him. "What do you mean?"

"With feeling running this high, we'll be lucky if they keep us."

"Of course they'll keep us. We've booked in till tomorrow. If not, I shall certainly complain. To the French National Tourist Office, and to Michelin and Baedeker and the Guides Bleus and anyone else you care to name."

"I'm sure you will," Peter said hastily, "but it won't solve the problem of tonight."

"There may not be a problem. Stop fretting," Dora commanded, her voice sharper because she was ill at ease.

However, she was right, as usual. She would be, Peter thought. At the Coq d'Or the proprietor had seen them coming. He came forward to greet them as they arrived.

"Bonsoir, madame . . . monsieur. . . . You have made your expedition? The whole village can talk of nothing else. It is not every day there is a visit to the island. I hope at least that you have no regrets?"

"None at all," Dora told him very firmly.

Peter allowed it to seem that she was speaking for them both.

"You see?" she said when they were alone together. "The proprietor made no difficulties. Hotel people are civilized and cosmopolitan. They have to be—it's part of their stock-in-trade. It just underlines the difference between them and these ignorant peasants. The proprietor isn't afraid to speak to us."

Nevertheless, it seemed to Peter that the proprietor was troubled. He had lost the easy manner of last night. He was politer than ever, even deferential, but there was a certain reserve in what he said. He kept his distance as though there was a physical barrier between them. At the bar, he did not join them for a drink. Instead, he stayed firmly behind the counter; it was as if he had walled himself in. He kept himself busy rearranging bottles and polishing glasses. There was no one else in the room.

It was Dora, of course, who opened the conversation.

"Who lives on the Island of Regrets?"

"No one, madame."

"But someone does. We met him. We both saw him. Unless you're going to say he was a ghost?"

"No, madame, there are no ghosts on the island."

"So he's a living person?"

The proprietor looked away.

"Isn't he?" Dora pursued. "After all, the boat calls with provisions. He must be as alive as you."

This time the proprietor faced her. "You have met this person, you say?"

Dora nodded.

"Then you will know that he is a madman. There is always a madman on the Ile des Regrets."

"How do you mean—there is always a madman?"

"It may sound strange, monsieur, but it is so."

"But who sends them there? Where do they come from?"

"That, monsieur, we do not know."

"It's fantastic," Dora burst out. "Such callousness, such indifference."

The proprietor was polishing a glass. "Every community has its share of such poor creatures," he said softly, "and always they must be put away. They are dangerous to themselves and to others. The incurables, as one might say—although beasts in cages would be a better description, since they must always be behind bars; and what bars could be more effective than to be cast away on the Ile des Regrets without a boat?"

"You mean they are left there to die?" Dora asked with horror.

"No, madame, our madmen live for many years. They are amply supplied with provisions. By tradition, the whole village contributes. And when one goes, another is always forthcoming—no one knows from where. One day the whisper spreads through the village: 'There's a new madman on the Ile des Regrets.' "

"And you send out a welcoming committee?"

"Monsieur will have his little joke." The proprietor was repolishing the glasses. "You must pardon that I am so *affairé*. We hear tonight that a big coach-party is coming and every bed will be in use. It does not happen often," he continued, as if aware of the thinness of the excuse, "but when it does, we are naturally very busy, since every room must be turned out."

Complete stillness reigned in the hotel; the bustle of room-turning-out was evidently over. The excuse was so patently transparent that Peter was tempted to smile. The proprietor, while aware of his duties as a hôtelier, was making sure they did not stay beyond tonight. Not only was some dreadful fate expected to overtake them, but they were regarded as bringers of bad luck. The whole of Kéroualhac ached to be without them, and they would never be welcomed back. This was therefore their last chance to probe the mystery surrounding the Ile des Regrets.

"What about that house on the island?" Peter demanded. "That could do with a bit of turning out."

It was the proprietor's turn to show a gleam of humour. "Madmen are not good housewives, as a rule."

"You're telling me," Dora broke in. "The place is filthy. How long has it been left to rot like that?"

"Since the owner built it," the proprietor answered. "He was another one who would not heed." He looked at them over the glass he was polishing for the third time. "Everyone told him that the Ile des Regrets was dangerous, but he did not choose to believe. He visited it, declared it to his liking, and decided to build a summer retreat. He had ample time to reflect upon our warnings during the years that he spent upon the Ile. He was rash enough to wish when he first set foot there that he might pass the rest of his life in this idyllic spot. As usual, his wish was granted and as usual it became a source of regret."

"What happened?" Dora demanded.

"His wife died first of all. She was being rowed across from the mainland by a boatman who had lived here all his life. Inexplicably, he misjudged the crossing. They were caught in the tide-rip and drowned.

"As if this were not sufficient sorrow, his daughter was taken from him that same year. One wing of the house was not yet completed. The child was playing there when a wall collapsed.

"Instead of leaving the scene of his bereavement, our island-dweller shut himself up in the house. He grew melancholy, neglected his financial enterprises; he made business trips to Paris less and less. He was a director of many companies, prosperous but not solid, except in build. The Stavisky scandal broke over him like a thunderstorm, for which he was completely unprepared. In a week his shares, like those of so many others, tumbled; his frantic speculations on the Bourse all failed. He returned to the island broken in mind and body. Within a week it was apparent he was mad. His servants in terror sought refuge on the mainland. He was left alone on his island. For fifteen years he lived there. When he died, another madman took his place."

"I don't understand—" Dora was beginning.

"No one understands, madame. One afternoon the boat-crew, unloading provisions, were hailed by a different man. No one knew where he had come from. To this day we do not know his name. He was succeeded by another, and another. The one you saw must be at least the sixth. Nor do we know how they get to the island in the first place, since no boatman has ever taken one across, but you have shown us, madame, that it is possible to hire or steal conveyance, and our madmen, who do not lack cunning, could easily have done as much."

"But how do they know when to go there?"

"How does the swallow know when to journey south? There are things, monsieur, that science does not answer. And now, my wife calls that your sole is cooked."

The proprietor came out from behind the bar-counter, not without a certain hesitation, Peter thought. And as he served the food and poured the wine, Peter noticed that the proprietor kept as much distance as he could between himself and his guests. Nor did the proprietor's wife issue forth after supper to receive their compliments on her cuisine, and the little chambermaid, seeing Dora coming, crossed herself and took to her heels. It was as though the whole village feared that disaster was going to strike them, some sudden death-in-agony in the night. Like the boy who had so rashly eaten blackberries on the island, and now lay in the churchyard with a twig of mountain ash on his grave. In this climate it was easy to see how superstition became established. The will to perceive causality was already there.

Next morning, when they came down safe and well to breakfast, Peter detected a slight disappointment in the air, mingled with relief that they were going and could therefore bring down no wrath on Kéroualhac. Not a soul was to be seen and yet all eyes were upon them as the proprietor himself saw them off in the direction of Brest and St. Malo.

During the next six months their recollection of the island faded as preparations for the wedding got under way. For Peter's sake, Mrs. Matthews had determined to speed things up; long engagements were bad for the nerves, she said.

Peter was indeed in a state of considerable nervous tension, but not for the reasons his future mother-in-law supposed. The impending union weighed heavily upon his spirit. He wished it were over, or else that it need never take place. But when he voiced his doubts to Dora she became tearful—an act in which long practice had made her adept—and rushed to confide in her mother, who discovered that April was a better month than June. Peter suffered her sympathetic misunderstanding with outward gratitude and inward rage. He displayed the same stoic self-control when enduring the banter of his colleagues at the Ministry of Ag. and Fish. He had little time to reflect—or, when he did, to ponder—on the events on the Ile des Regrets. As for Dora, the island would have passed out of her memory completely had it not been for the vexing business of the snaps.

Every one of the snapshots she had taken on the island came out blank. The chemist's assistant talked knowingly about a faulty shutter, but the camera, when examined, was all right. Nor was Dora a tyro photographer, unused to light-readings and the like, or one who forgot to wind the film after each exposure or failed to take it out of the camera with care. The chemist's assistant maintained that he had not been negligent; he and Dora united in blaming the film; but the manufacturers, to whom Dora complained energetically, replied after six weeks that it was not their fault. The film had been tested in their laboratories and had emerged with flying colours. No other in that batch had been reported faulty and they could therefore accept no liability. They added, in what read like an afterthought, that the film appeared to have been exposed to strong white light. Dora crumpled the letter angrily when she received it and refused to have the matter mentioned any more.

Three weeks before the wedding, which was at Easter, Dora went down with a cold, caught while preening in her wedding-dress in an unheated bedroom before the only full-length mirror in the house. The cold made her feel heavy and miserable; her temperature began to rise. Despite a couple of days in bed and endless aspirins, the indisposition failed to respond.

The doctor, when he came (rushed off his feet by a measles epidemic), was not unduly alarmed by Dora's case. He satisfied himself that she had not got pneumonia, and departed, leaving a prescription behind. Peter fetched the prescription from the chemist — the same chemist who had developed the photographs — and was served by the same assistant, a small black-bearded young man. Peter thought he glanced at him accusingly as the white-wrapped sealed package changed hands, but he dismissed this as due to his imagination; it was not his fault that Dora was ill.

And ill she was. No one could accuse her of malingering. Her temperature had continued to rise. At 101 degrees it was not dangerous, but it steadfastly refused to come down. Dora herself seemed fretful and restless, suffering now here, now there. So many of her organs seemed in turn to be affected that it was tempting to seek some psychosomatic cause. The doctor called again, looked baffled, and remained cheerful, though there was no doubt his patient had lost a lot of weight. A BCG test for tuberculosis proved negative. Even so, the doctor's cheerfulness did not fade. Dora, he assured her mother and her fiancé, was one of the healthiest young women he knew, and as usual when the healthy succumbed to illness, they were apt to worry and make recovery slow. He had no doubt that Dora's disease was due to a virus—exactly which he was not prepared to say. The viruses, like the Joneses, were so numerous as to defy classification; from uniformity came diversity. He suggested that Dora should go into the hospital for observation and admitted that the wedding might have to be put off.

Dora wept when the suggestion was put to her. She had made up her mind to be an Easter bride. Her mother and the doctor tried to soothe her. Peter felt guiltily that he ought to do the same, but his half-hearted attempts were so unsuccessful that Mrs. Matthews ordered him from the room. On the landing he paced up and down uncertainly, a prey to the conflict of his thoughts.

Dora did not improve in hospital; instead she grew steadily worse. Wasted, feverish, and hollow-cheeked, she was scarcely recognizable. The wedding was indefinitely postponed.

It was while Peter was visiting her that she dropped her bombshell. She put her burning hand in his and said: "Darling, I'm not getting better—I'm not going to. It's because we went to that wretched Ile des Regrets."

"Nonsense, Dora," Peter said sharply. "What are you talking about?"

"I don't know." Her eyes filled with tears—of weakness this time. "It's just the way I feel about it all."

"Sick fancies," Peter said with attempted heartiness. "You'll be as right as rain very soon."

"But they don't even know what's the matter with me. A virus disease can mean anything."

"Or nothing," Peter tried to reassure her. "You mustn't upset yourself like this."

"No," Dora agreed with unaccustomed meekness. "Only I keep thinking about that wish."

"What wish?" Peter demanded.

"The wish that I made on the island—that I might believe in magic. Like you."

Peter also had expressed a wish on the island, though he preferred not to think about it now.

"I don't see any connection between your wish and your illness," he objected.

"But there is." Dora lowered her head in confusion. "I believe in magic now."

The icy fingers on Peter's spine made him shiver. Without conviction, he said: "You're being a bit extreme, like all converts. This could be coincidence."

"No." Dora shook her head with something of her old vigour. "I've never been ill like this. It's like that boy who ate blackberries on the island, except that his was mercifully quick."

"And you're not dying," Peter said with what cheerfulness he could muster. "And you didn't have anything to eat. Or did you?" he asked, alarmed by Dora's silence.

"No, Peter, I ate nothing."

And then it all came out in a torrent of self-justification. She had taken something from the Island of Regrets. "Only a fir-cone, Peter, like the ones I was pelting you with. And I never intended taking it. It must have fallen into my bag. I didn't find it until two nights later in the hotel at St. Malo, and then I said nothing to you."

"What did you do with it, then?"

"Nothing, darling. I brought it home and put it in a drawer."

"You mean you've still got it?" Peter demanded with sudden excitement.

"Yes. It's in the top drawer of my desk. Unless Mummy's tidied it away," Dora added. "She does sometimes. But it was there before I fell ill—I saw it. It's opened a bit but it's otherwise perfectly preserved."

Peter stood up. "In that case, we must return it."

"Do you think that will do any good?"

"It won't do any harm, and your doctors are not being successful. Restoring the fir-cone is your only chance."

"But there's no postal service to the island. And no one from Kéroualhac would go."

"If you like, I'll take it," Peter offered.

Dora made objections, but allowed them to be overruled. She gave him instructions where to find the fir-cone, and Peter went at once to her house. Mrs. Matthews looked startled and not too pleased to see him, but she held the door open none the less.

"What is it? Is Dora worse?" she demanded as soon as Peter had stepped into the hall.

Peter shook his head and explained his mission: Dora wanted something from her desk.

"Why didn't she ask me to bring it?" her mother protested.

"She only thought of it just now."

"It must be very urgent if it couldn't wait till tomorrow."

"It *is* urgent," Peter assured her. "It's a matter of life and death."

She followed him reluctantly to Dora's bedroom, where the desk was kept unlocked. It was a walnut Queen-Anne-style model with small drawers that pulled out sideways, but there was no fir-cone in any of them. Peter began to poke about among the papers stuffed into pigeonholes above the writing flap.

Mrs. Matthews watched him in silence, like a professional burglar assessing an amateur's attempts. "If I knew what you were looking for . . ." she suggested.

"I'm looking for a fir-cone," Peter said.

"A fir-cone!" Mrs. Matthews's voice was remarkably like her daughter's. "You're not going to tell me that Dora sent you here to pick up that?"

"It has sentimental associations," Peter said lamely.

"A fir-cone, indeed! I can tell you, you won't find that."

"You mean you know where it is?" Peter asked hopefully.

"I put it in the dustbin last week."

"What!" Peter spun round, leaving the desk-drawers gaping. "What in heaven's name possessed you to do that?"

"I take it I may act as I wish in my own home," Mrs. Matthews reproved him. "Dora is my daughter, after all."

"That doesn't give you the right to dispose of her belongings. Couldn't you have waited till she was dead?"

"Peter!"

"I'm sorry. I didn't mean it. Forgive me."

"My poor boy, you're thoroughly overwrought." Such demented distress was so flattering to Dora that Mrs. Matthews was prepared to be generous in return.

But Peter ignored her generosity. "Which day does your dustman call?"

"Tuesday morning," Mrs. Matthews answered.

"Then there's just a chance that the fir-cone is still there."

He was already on his way to the kitchen when Dora's mother succeeded in catching his arm. "Peter, listen. I know you hate to disappoint her, but there's no point in turning my dustbin upside down. The fir-cone won't be any use if you find it. It was mouldy. Rotten to the core."

With a cry, Peter broke away from her. "Are you certain?"

"Of course I am. That's why I threw it away. You don't really think I'd dispose of Dora's things for no reason?"

"But she told me the fir-cone was all right."

"I expect she hadn't looked at it lately."

The sweat was standing out on Peter's brow. "I've got to have it," he cried. "Oh, God, I've got to have it."

He made a dive towards the kitchen-door. There was a clatter as the dustbin was up-ended. The refuse rolled in all directions over the yard. Mrs. Matthews watched with mingled alarm and horror as Peter, unheeding, flung himself on his knees among the cinders, tin cans, withered flowers, empty bottles, and rotting cabbage-leaves.

Even so, he almost missed the fir-cone, which had rolled as if trying to escape. Then he spied it and rose, stained but triumphant.

Dora's mother looked at him pityingly. "You see? It's exactly as I told you—not worth keeping. Dora won't want to have it now. In fact, I doubt if the hospital would allow it. It's not a very hygienic souvenir."

Something about the fir-cone's soft, rotting substance made Peter's gorge rise until he wanted to retch. He fought down the nausea with an effort. It was as though his fingers had touched decaying flesh.

He put it in his pocket and turned to Dora's mother. "I'll take it back," he said in a hollow-sounding voice.

"I should leave it till the morning," she said gently. "They won't let you see Dora now."

"No, no. I don't mean to Dora. I mean I'm taking it to the Ile des Regrets."

To Peter, that evening was the beginning of a nightmare. It proved impossible to book a seat on a plane. The Easter holiday rush had already started and there was nothing for it but to travel by boat and train. But he had already missed the night boat from Southampton and he could not afford another twenty-four hours' delay. The fir-cone in his pocket seemed to be mouldering faster. Eventually he settled for the crossing Newhaven-Dieppe. From Dieppe he could travel cross-country to Quimper, and from Quimper by bus to Kéroualhac. He did not know how he would cross from there to the island, but trusted that he would find some means of accomplishing this last lap. He would beg, buy, borrow, even steal a boat if need be. Desperation would show him the way. The fir-cone had to be returned if Dora's death were not to be on his conscience, for had he not wished that their marriage might never take place? Admittedly he had not wished that any disaster should befall Dora and nothing had been further from his thoughts; but it was the way of the Ile des Regrets to grant a wish and cause one to regret its granting — as Dora regretted being ill.

At the thought of that mysterious malady, Peter's scalp prickled. Dora, like the fir-cone, was rapidly wasting away. Unless he could return it in time, he knew too well what would happen. And now, when he most needed speed, he encountered only adversity and delay.

The Channel was rough and the boat was an hour late on the crossing, which meant he had missed his connection with the fast train. At St. Malo a porter gave him wrong information and allowed his train to pull out under his nose. The excited Englishman in a

stained suit, unshaven, untidy, speaking unintelligible French, was
an object of mirth rather than of pity to this Breton, who, when he
understood the purport of his questions, amused himself with
overliteral replies. No, there were no more trains until tomorrow.
The last bus? That had left an hour ago. There would not be another
till Saturday. A daily service? *Bien sûr* there was a daily service, but it
did not run on the Friday before Easter, of course. Yes, monsieur
could hire a car if he preferred it, and no, the garage was not open
this afternoon. And who had said anything about there being no
means of getting to Quimper? Monsieur had been asking about
getting there *direct*. But if he took a bus to La Rocaille and there
changed to another bus, he could be in Quimper by half-past four
tonight. Only the bus for La Rocaille was on the point of departure;
one would telephone and ask it to wait. . . .

It was when he was on the bus and had got his breath back that
Peter first saw the Face. Small and malignant, it leered at him from a
peasant-woman's market-basket and seemed to require some leer or
gesture in return. Its expression was one of malicious satisfaction, as
though it were pleased that the journey was late and slow. Yet when
Peter moved his head in an effort to escape its triumph and looked
again at the basket, it was no longer there.

Thereafter it played hide-and-seek with him among the
passengers; it peered at him from over the shoulder of the man in
front; it grimaced at him from the crook of a woman's arm hung with
parcels; where two children put their heads together and whispered,
it made an evil and, to all but Peter, invisible third.

It vanished each time he moved abruptly on the narrow seat, to the
discomfort of his neighbour who glared at him with such intense
ferocity that Peter felt impelled to explain.

"*Il y a quelquechose dans le panier de cette dame-là,*" he murmured.

"*Et vous, vous avez quelquechose dans le cul.*"

Between dread of seeing the Face and mortification, Peter did not
know which way to look. No one else seemed to have perceived this
grotesque, non-fare-paying passenger. Peter began to wonder if he

was imagining things; he had slept very little on the crossing. . . .
And then the Face put out its tongue at him.

Quick as lightning, Peter returned the compliment, only to meet
the horrified then angry gaze of the woman opposite. She gave a
small, involuntary scream. Peter's neighbour cautioned him to mind
his manners. Any trouble and they would put him off the bus, him
and his remarks about "something in the market-basket." Just let
him try anything with Madame Blanche, that was all.

In vain Peter protested that his gesture was not intended for the
lady. The whole bus looked at him in pity and scorn. "*Mais voyons!*"
his self-appointed gaoler-neighbour expostulated, "there is only
Madame Blanche who sits there. Therefore you intended to insult
her. Whom else could you have intended to insult?" And the other
passengers joined with the Face in looking at him accusingly all the
way to La Rocaille.

The second bus was waiting in the town square. It appeared in-
credibly old. The windows did not fit, and they bumped and rattled
as the bus threaded its way over La Rocaille's cobblestones. The
woman with the market-basket was no longer with them, but as he
turned to look at the landscape, Peter saw with a shudder of fear that
the Face still was. Only now it had been joined by other Faces. There
was a whole row of them above the electric lights. They grinned and
gibbered, put out their tongues and made long noses, leered and
winked at him in an obscene, revolting way. He passed a hand across
his eyes, and found it wet with perspiration. The sweat was standing
out in beads upon his brow.

"Stop the bus and let me off," he commanded.

Someone behind asked if he felt all right.

"Yes. No. I want to get off," Peter repeated.

Impossible, the bus was late already, he was told. There was no
time to wait for someone to puke by the roadside. From somewhere
his fellow passengers produced a stout brown-paper bag.

"But I don't feel sick!" Peter protested emphatically.

"You wanted to stop the bus."

"Only so that I could get out and walk a little. Away from those Faces up there."

He jerked his head in the direction of the light-bulbs, three of which had failed to come on. His fellow passengers followed the gesture blankly. It was evident they saw nothing there. One or two of them tapped their foreheads significantly. The woman behind Peter ostentatiously moved away. Only his gaoler-neighbour seemed unaffected. Peter wondered if he could see the Faces too. He concentrated on staring out of the window at the countryside, still desolate after a late cold spring, while the row of Faces looked down with their air of malicious triumph, whose cause he was to discover soon enough.

A few miles from Quimper the bus stopped with a particularly bone-shaking rattle, and the driver-conductor got down. He walked, bandy-legged but purposeful, towards the radiator, unscrewed the cap, and let off a head of steam. *"Encore une fois,"* Peter heard the other passengers whispering all around him. It was evidently not a rare event. The driver leaned negligently against the bonnet, while clouds of steam rose into the evening air. From somewhere he had produced a can of water; he had also produced a cigarette. The passengers inside were likewise furnished. Everyone seemed prepared for a wait. And through the window Peter could catch a glimpse of the sea in the distance, sullen and heaving, and the tide was coming in.

In another hour the tide would make the channel between Kéroualhac and the island impassable. And after that, darkness would descend and he would be subject to another night's delay. In vain Peter tapped his feet and fidgeted with impatience, drumming his fingers on the rattling window-pane. Through it he could see the line of white which broke against a headland, and watch its progress, whipped by the wind, along the shore. If he looked inwards, he could see the mocking Faces, whose mockery was reserved for him alone. One of them in particular had descended from the ceiling and hovered a little way to the left of him in the air. The tongue ran over the lips in anticipation as they pursed themselves, ready to spit. . . .

With a cry, Peter struck out at this monstrosity, an ill-aimed buffet which caught his gaoler-neighbour's lighted cigarette, knocking the glowing stub among the other passengers in an avalanche of swearing and stamping it out.

"Can't you save your tricks until you're back among the inmates?" the angry victim exclaimed. "I could report you to the gendarmes for this one. You a pyromaniac, or what?"

"I beg your pardon," Peter murmured in English.

"English, *hein?* We know that the English are mad. But, *sacré nom!* why can't you go mad on your side of the Channel? Don't you know that's what the English Channel's for?"

Peter's answer (if he made one) was lost in the revving of the engine. The bus, recuperated, moved off with a spine-jarring jerk. Through the window he could see that the line of white around the headland had devoured a good deal more of the shore.

At Kéroualhac he was one of the first passengers to alight. The bus had stopped outside the Coq d'Or, which, as yet not open for the summer, presented a shuttered, cloistered front to the main street. Pausing only to note this inhospitable welcome, Peter sought the short cut to the harbour through the churchyard. Here there was no lack of hospitality. An open grave, boarded over, yawned near the path. The Faces, whom Peter had temporarily forgotten, peered at him round the corner of the church. In his pocket, where his hand stole now and then for reassurance, the fir-cone seemed deliquescent to his touch.

As he came out of the churchyard into the harbour, he became aware for the first time of the baying of the sea. It kept up a continuous worrying of the weed-covered rocks and the sea-wall, like hounds who have cornered a beast and are holding him at bay. The few boats drawn up on the hard were beached in safety. The fishing fleet had not left port today. The only sign of life was a dinghy chugging its way across the harbour, piloted by an oilskinned and sou'westered man.

Peter leaned against the harbour wall and feigned interest in the water, watching the man out of the corner of his eye. There was no other boat he could use to reach the island, and his chances of hiring it seemed small. No boatman would venture outside the harbour, let alone entrust his boat to someone else, for within the next half-hour the tide-rip would block the channel to the island; it was already dangerous to attempt to cross.

The man in oilskins seemed unaware of Peter's presence. He made fast the dinghy to a ring in the harbour wall and scaled the iron ladder from the water, leaving his boat bobbing below. He had stripped off his heavy oilskins for ease of movement and he wore the usual seaman's jersey underneath. A local fisherman, Peter thought — perhaps one of those who had been hostile when he and Dora returned from visiting the Ile des Regrets.

As the man approached Peter, he stared curiously. It was too early in the year for visitors.

Peter, feeling that some remark was called for, could think only of inanities.

"A bad day," he volunteered with a glance towards the fishing fleet in harbour.

"Not unusual at this time of year."

The fisherman was passing without so much as a second glance in his direction when Peter remarked: "Not much activity here today."

"Ah, monsieur, you come at a time of sorrow. We mourn the death of one of our best-loved men. I knew him all my life. He was like a brother. And now he is drowned, God rest him, and to be buried in the morning. It is sad when a man must carry his best friend to the grave."

"The storm must have been a very bad one."

"He was not drowned in the storm. He was drowned here in the harbour in calm water by the boat of his on which there was a curse. We urged him to get rid of her, but he was stubborn. He laughed at us for believing in bad luck. But last night the boat, a dinghy like mine with an outboard motor, capsized near the harbour mouth. The motor struck Yves on the head as he went under. He was dead by the time we got him out. In all my days I have never known a dinghy capsize like that one. There was no reason for it, except that the thing was accursed."

"What do you mean?" Peter asked uneasily.

"A stranger would not understand, monsieur."

"No," Peter insisted, "please explain. I am interested."

"It has to do with the island in the bay, the Ile des Regrets, as we call it. The place is unlucky; no one from Kéroualhac will go there. Yves no more than the rest. But last summer a young English couple of more than usual stupidity helped themselves to Yves's boat, which thus spent some hours on the island. The boat has been accursed ever since."

"And the couple? What happened to the English couple?" Peter tried to keep the urgency out of his voice.

"I don't know, but I hope they have not gone unpunished. Since they have caused a death, they deserve to atone."

"No!" Peter cried, and was astonished at his own vehemence. "One of them has atoned enough. She lies sick of an illness that has defeated all her doctors, and unless I can reach the island tonight she will die."

"It would be madness to try to reach the island," the fisherman warned him. "Apart from ill-luck, the tide is almost at its height." He had already stepped between Peter and the sea-wall, as if to protect his boat.

"I will pay you good money to hire your dinghy," Peter promised.

"Think I'd ever see my boat again in this sea? Or that I'd ever want to after she'd been to the island? No, monsieur, there's not a man in Kéroualhac will help you in getting there."

"In that case I shall have to help myself," Peter retorted.

"It's suicide," the fisherman warned him grimly.

Peter's hand closed round the fir-cone as he thought of Dora. "It will be more like murder if I don't."

The man looked at him strangely, without blinking, and Peter recognized suddenly and with blinding clarity that here was the original of the Face. The lips were not pursed now to spit forth contumely; the expression seemed rather to be one of malicious glee.

As Peter watched, the mouth began to stretch and widen until the lips were taut and distorted as an extended rubber band. The eyes, which were narrow and near together, seemed almost to be buried in the flesh. With a cry of horror, Peter lunged at the mask before him and heard rather than felt his knuckles connect with bone. He had no clear idea of what it was he was destroying; he knew only that destroy he must.

The fisherman went down like a ninepin. Peter, not normally a fighter, was suddenly shocked and appalled. His first instinct was to offer aid and explanation. His second to make for the boat. The second won, for already the fisherman was dazedly stirring. Then, as he saw Peter disappearing over the iron ladder, he gave a great shout and began to struggle to his feet. Peter's fingers wrestled clumsily with the moorings. He cast off the rope just in time. As the fisherman's head appeared over the sea-wall, the boat began to glide away. The fisherman yelled something unintelligible and minatory. Peter stood up, his movement rocking the boat. He fumbled in his breast-pocket and produced his wallet, still stuffed with worn thousand-franc notes.

"Here!" he shouted, as a sea-gull screamed in derision. "I don't want to steal your boat." And he hurled the wallet with all his might towards the quayside, where it landed with a satisfying thump.

The fisherman, whose face seemed to have reverted to a normal Breton peasant's, gazed from Peter to the wallet, but made no attempt to pick the latter up. Then, with a shrug of massive resignation and a glance all around at the empty wastes of the sea, he made off as fast as sea-booted legs would carry him. He crossed himself before he turned away.

Outside the harbour the waves began in earnest. The sea-bed seemed to be tilting this way and that. The waves did not break, but slid smoothly towards the coastline, intent on trying to vanquish its battered rock. Sea and land were locked in a sempiternal struggle in which countless vessels had been sacrificed to no effect. It seemed too much to hope that a dinghy might survive it, but to Peter's relief it did. After he had got used to the long glide over the surface of a shoreward-mounting swell and the heart-stopping moment at its conclusion when another wave reared up ahead, he began to realize that the dinghy (for the moment) could take it better perhaps than a bigger boat. He calculated the distance to the island. He might yet do it in time.

But the wind and water were against him. His progress was maddeningly slow. The tide, frothing in the channel, had made the water-level dangerously high. Without warning, the sea began to boil all around him, the wind and waves contending with the tide. The water, compressed into swirling eddies, began to race with the speed of an express train. The dinghy, almost on the shoreward side of safety, was borne broadside, parallel to the isle. In vain Peter struggled to turn her bows into the tide-rip. She heeled over, righted herself, heeled over, further over, and overturned. Peter had a glimpse of her, carried keel upwards towards the jagged rocks at the island's harbour mouth. Then the sea propelled him in the same direction, and he struggled desperately to keep himself afloat.

The wave which flung him finally shorewards was one of the largest yet to break. The impact knocked all the breath out of his body, but at least he fell on sand. The sand was smooth, sliding treacherously beneath his fingers, until he realized he was caught in the undertow. Panting, heaving, straining to gain some purchase, his scrabbling fingers encountered a furrowed slab of rock. His hands were so numb that he could scarcely distinguish rock and fingers. Sea-water streaming down his face left him choking and half-blind. And then another drenching wave broke over him, and again he had to fight the undertow.

This time, by an effort he had believed beyond him, he dragged himself beyond the ocean's clawing reach. Spewing sea-water and retching his heart out, he lay prone and shivering among rock pools and seaweed, too terrified and exhausted even to think.

It was the cold that brought him to his senses. He was cold within and without. But surprisingly, his legs responded to his summons. Dizzily, staggering with the effort, he forced himself to his feet. There was blood on his hands and on his forehead where he had cut himself upon the rocks. His trousers flapped sodden and heavy about him. In the maelstrom his shoes had been sucked off. Behind him was a waste of whirling water, racing like a river in flood. Before him lay the now sharply remembered horrors he had encountered on the Island of Regrets.

At least, Peter thought, wringing the water from his garments, I have not made a wish this time. And that thought reminded him of the fir-cone. Suppose, in that wild sea, it had been washed away? But no! It was safely there in an inner pocket, no more pulpy than everything else he possessed. He beat his arms to restore some vestige of circulation, and set off inland towards the wood.

The path by the stream was spiked with reeds and marshy, with a green-tinged, evil-smelling ooze. His feet sank in above the ankles, his trouser-legs became solid with the slime. The stream which had babbled so delightfully now ran silent, swollen into flood. From the bushes no birds sang, despite the season. The light was beginning to fail.

In the pine-wood it was darker still and more silent. A curious stillness prevailed. Peter almost preferred the desolation of bare branches to the pine-trees' sinister, everlasting life. He found the tree without difficulty from which the fir-cone had come. Other fir-cones lay on the damp, decaying needles. Reverently he laid his down. Its mildewed, water-logged appearance made it easy to recognize, yet when he looked a moment later, it had vanished clean away.

At once there was laughter all around him, thin, shrill laughter which had a spiteful ring. At first he thought it was the madman, but it lacked the raucous cackling of his cries. Besides, this was not one laugh but many. A chorus of malice echoed among the trees. And then he saw the Faces all around him, peering from behind tree-trunks, in the branches, even in the air at the level of his eyes.

Awkwardly in his bare feet and sea-sodden garments, Peter began to run. He ran downhill because it was the way he was facing, and also because a house was at least somewhere to go. The tenant might be mad—that did not matter. He was a fellow human-being after all. Anything was better than the company of the unseen dwellers on the island. Almost sobbing with relief, Peter pounded the solid oak of the front door.

It swung inwards, and he saw at a glance that nothing was different, except that the place was damper and exuded a musty smell. In the drawing-room some plaster had fallen from the ceiling and a strip of wall-paper was peeling from the wall. The whole house was even more silent than he remembered and had a curiously dank and vaultlike chill. Or was it merely that he was soaked to the skin and shaken by rigors in every member? In the hope of attracting his weird host's attention, he pulled long and violently at the bell.

Silence. And after silence, more silence, welling in the dark on the heels of retreating light. In the hope that the madman might have kindled a fire, Peter made his way to the kitchen, but a glance at the ashes in the grate snuffed out his hopes. On a shelf stood several tins of food, unopened, but here also the dust lay thick. A plate in the sink contained some rock-hard unidentifiable substance which might have been edible once.

Peter peered out into the garden. The brown grass had been beaten to the ground by the fury of the winter storms that swept over the island. Of the madman there was no sign. Peter consoled himself by reflecting that the man might have been removed to a lunatic asylum on the mainland, though he knew in his heart this was not true. He shouted once or twice, but the only answer was silence. Not even an echo gave back his halloo.

Frightened more and more by this atmosphere of lurking evil, Peter made his way up the stairs. They groaned as though deploring his passage, which left a trail of water everywhere. The first bedroom he came to was empty, bare even of furniture. Two others, shrouded in cobwebs, opened off a corridor. At the far end was another doorway, masked by a moth-eaten portière. It crumbled and tore in Peter's fingers as he pulled it to one side and went in — and came face to face with the madman, propped up in a foully disordered bed. It took several seconds for him to realize that the staring eyes were sightless and that the madman, in fact, was dead.

The shock stopped his breath for a moment. When he exhaled, it was with a hoarse, choking scream. He turned and blundered blindly down the corridor, away from the hideous sight. But at the turn of the stairs a further shock awaited him. Confronting him was the madman's ghost. Wild-eyed, white hair disordered, the pallid face streaked with grime, the lips drawn back into a taut, tetanic rictus, the creature stood awaiting him. Peter threw up his hands in horror and the madman raised his arms to draw him in. There was a magnetism about his red-rimmed eyeballs. Against his will, Peter found himself advancing towards the outstretched arms. His own hands were outstretched to defend himself against the horror which left him powerless in every limb. Yet his legs continued to bear him forward and the madman to hold out his arms.

Peter knew that the creature's touch would be icy, but he was not prepared for quite such burning cold. Involuntarily his hands withdrew from the contact, and the madman's arms fell to his sides. For an instant the two men confronted each other. Then Peter Quint began to laugh. His mirror image joined him in insane peals of grim amusement. "The new tenant, ha-ha-ha!"

Whether Peter had always been mentally unstable, or whether the shock of Dora's death sent him over the edge, has been hotly debated by his and her relations, but neither Peter nor Dora care. Both in their different ways are past all caring — Dora in the tomb and Peter in a home, where his relations expeditiously placed him as soon as his condition became known. The proprietor of the Coq d'Or will tell their story with very little prompting from his guests, who find it makes an excellent *apéritif*. There is a new madman on the Island of Regrets.

THE HARE

THE PATH THROUGH THE PINE-WOOD WAS NARROW AND STEEP AND silent. No birds sang and the needles underfoot made a soft, absorbent cushion of sound. Nothing grew, not even undergrowth, among the slim, scaly trunks of the pine-trees, and no light filtered through. Only the path itself was dappled with sunlight and allowed an occasional glimpse of the May sky overhead. The path zig-zagged wildly up the hillside, but it was still the shortest distance between two points.

Between East and West, Karlheinz Ackermann was thinking as he strode steadily and purposefully ahead. Who knew what understanding might be reached, what bargain struck as a result of his mission? Or rather, of his response to these feelers from the other side. And to think that it should all take place here, in these Harz Mountains where he had spent so many boyhood holidays, so that not only did he know the forest paths as well as most of the locals, but his return to childhood haunts caused no surprise. True, Tante Berthe and Tante Lise were no longer living, but after the war, who heeded individual death? And how touching that their only nephew,

Karlheinz, now forty, whom many people remembered in Lederhosen, should still feel drawn to visiting the town.

"So unassuming," they said, "and him a colonel." Karlheinz, hearing them, smiled. They would have been still more astonished had they known the nature of his duties — but no one except his chief knew that. The Abwehr, the West German intelligence service; many people, he supposed, would say he was a spy. Even today, when he was keeping an East German appointment, it was his duty to observe and discover all he could. "Even the swallows are late again this year" — that was the password; but whether the speaker would be man or woman, young or old, Karlheinz did not know, nor where on this forest path he would encounter the unknown emissary who had important information to impart.

It would not be within the next five minutes — of that he was certain, for the path stretched emptily ahead. Already he could see the light through the trees where the brow of this first hill waited, and, looking back at the tree-trunks suspiciously crowding behind him, he had the impression of emerging from a noonday night.

When he reached the brow of the hill the panorama was unexpected. The hill was not high enough to warrant such a view, but it was so placed that to the east no major height rose up in front of it, and the surrounding tree-clad hills were plain to see. Steep, rounded, and getting steadily higher to the eastwards, with here and there one of distinctive shape, and all climbing mistily towards the Brocken, which stood out, easily overtopping the others, a high splendid ridge with an observation tower on top.

And the Brocken, which he had climbed so often, was in East Germany — a country ethnically, geographically, linguistically the same, but divided by an arbitrary "frontier" hacked out among the pine-trees, mined, swept by machine-guns, and patrolled by dogs and men. It was incomprehensible and horrible, like the railway-line in the town station that had been torn up. Once the line had wound and twisted its way towards other small towns set deep among the mountains; now these lay beyond that pale-green swathe of cut-down forest which neither men, nor motor-cars, nor railway lines could cross.

Yet someone was going to cross it. Karlheinz felt his scalp tingle with excitement. There must be secret paths across the frontier zone. Even now, perhaps, a bare two miles away some man was darting from shadowy tree-trunk to tree-trunk, trying to make himself look shadowy too. And he had presumably made it, for no gunfire had rent the afternoon, whereas sometimes, when the wind was in the right direction and the East German guards were jumpy, the rattle of their machine-guns could be clearly heard.

Karlheinz looked again towards the Brocken, rising remote and tantalizingly out of reach. Involuntarily his hands clenched; it was still his country, still Germany, but only the witches on Walpurgis Night could get there now; and perhaps not even West German broomsticks could make it, for clear in the sunlight he could see a patch of snow glinting on the top. Of course it had been a long, hard winter, but everyone knew that on Walpurgis Night the witches swept the last of the snow away. And now, three weeks later, it still lay there. Perhaps only half the coven had been able to convene.

He wondered what the East German guards would do if they saw a witch ride over on her broomstick. Probably shoot her down, and then have difficulty explaining it afterwards. He smiled, envisaging the scene. Just so would his own superiors have acted when he was a young officer in the last inglorious days of the Third Reich.

Now some of those superiors were high-ranking officers in East Germany, owing different political allegiance, but basically quite unchanged. And others were dead: in Normandy and the Ardennes, on the vast plains of Russia, under the skies of Africa and Italy, while he, Karlheinz, had survived to become the contact man in West Germany for one of these same senior officers who wanted to defect to the West.

"It may be a bluff," Karlheinz's chief had warned him, "or it may be something big. And you're in it on your own to start with. I don't want to be brought in."

Karlheinz nodded and licked his lips. He knew the signs of danger. His heart began to thud irregularly. If it was indeed a bluff and he was captured, he could expect no communication or help. The Abwehr was about to disown him — he had seen it happen before with other agents who had set out on missions and for the most part had failed to return. Sometimes he wondered if it was a device for getting rid of unwanted agents. One slip, one failure was too much; yet men who knew so many secrets could not be allowed to retire into obscurity; a third alternative had to be found. Karlheinz had even wondered if these disappearances were not by arrangement with the Communists, a kind of reciprocal elimination campaign. But all he knew was that on this twenty-fifth of May, between three and three-thirty, along a stretch of forest path some two miles long, he would be greeted by an emissary with a password: "Even the swallows are late again this year."

The hare which started up almost at his feet frightened him so much that it made him angry. Damn the beast for startling him like that! What was it doing, so near a path in broad daylight, and deep in a pine-wood so far away from grass? It was a large hare, one of the largest Karlheinz remembered seeing, and it bounded away up the slope with long, leisurely leaps nowhere near the limit of its agility; yet it moved with astonishing speed. Its great round full eye was on him, lustrous with terror. He had time to notice that it had shed its winter coat and assumed the dun-coloured pelt of summer. And then, in a flash, it had gone.

Karlheinz reflected that his nerves were so fine-drawn that if a mouse had squeaked he would have started. His hand went involuntarily to the short, brutal knife fixed to the inside of his sleeve and concealed by the lining. It was good to depend on something other than one's wits. He was beginning to regret the hare, so plump and juicy; if he had had a gun he could have fired and presented his trophy proudly to the hotel kitchen; they would have been delighted to serve him a thick roast saddle of hare.

And now the pine-trees were thinning again as he walked downhill to a clearing — a field, the first of many fields. The grass was bright and already almost knee-high as he skirted it, consoled by the fact that his were not the first destructive steps. Several people seemed to have passed that way already, although he had heard no sound.

Then, as he turned a corner, he came upon them: a man and a woman making love. The man wore peasant clothes, the girl was hidden, except for a tangle of hair and a shapely leg.

Karlheinz stood still, swept first by embarrassment, and then, as the peasant raised a belligerent, steaming face and a little more of the girl was uncovered, by rising envy and lust. Her bodice was unlaced, her blouse had slipped from her shoulder, and her hair spread out around her head like golden snakes; and he knew before she opened them that her eyes would be as blue as flax-flowers and as clear as a mountain stream. It angered him that this peasant should enjoy anything so beautiful; but she should have known better than to give herself as cheaply as that. And with so little ceremony! Surely they could have gone further from the path? He was no prude, but even so there were limits. . . . The peasant began to rise aggressively to his feet.

"Seen all you want to see?"

The girl's arm pulled him down. Her eyes were open now, and Karlheinz noted that they were quite as blue as he expected. He noticed something else, too; they were as cold as marble, not glazed with passion or drowsy with contentment, and they were long and narrow, beautifully set above high cheek-bones — the eyes of someone from the eastern borders, where the blood was very slightly Slav.

"You're wasting time," Karlheinz heard her murmur. "It's getting late and I shall have to go."

The peasant hesitated a moment, and the girl wriggled from under him and raised herself on one arm.

"What's the use of you two fighting," she entreated, "when time passes and I was late getting here? Everything's late this spring; the trees aren't yet in full leaf nor the fields alight with flowers. Even the swallows are late again this year."

Her arguments seemed to convince the peasant, who fell back on her, greedily fumbling for her breasts. Karlheinz saw a slender arm pull him closer, and stayed to see no more.

The words she had spoken rang in his head like hammer-blows on an anvil. *Even the swallows are late again this year.* Was this lewd local wench the unknown emissary, or had some quirk of fate led her to use that phrase? Surely a girl like that could not cross a ferociously defended frontier where fear of a national getting out was balanced by fear of an alien getting in? Did that blonde head carry secret plans, the name of a high-ranking officer? He walked on blindly, uncertain of what to do next.

Within the next half-mile the stretch of path appointed for the meeting ended, and he could see no sign of anyone to meet; there was no form gliding among the trees or lurking in scant undergrowth. He became increasingly convinced that the rendezvous was a bluff, a decoy. For some reason the East Germans had wanted to know where he was that afternoon, perhaps to kidnap him? He felt himself come out in a cold sweat.

A twig snapping behind him so startled him that his hand went instinctively to his knife. He spun round and found himself facing the girl, her skirt crumpled, but otherwise none the worse.

Smiling, she indicated his gesture. "You will not need your knife, unless it is your custom to attack women who come to you alone and unarmed."

"Not if they behave themselves," Karlheinz said slowly. He was astonished to hear the menace in his voice, and wondered if the girl recognized, as he did, that the connotation of "behaving" was a sexual one.

"And if they don't?" she asked, still smiling.

"They are taught to. In various ways."

"What about unpunctuality — is that punished?"

Karlheinz glanced at his watch. "You aren't late," he said grudgingly.

"No, but the swallows are, aren't they? The swallows are late again this year."

She was offering her credentials to reassure him — more plainly this second time.

"I had not noticed the swallows," Karlheinz said pointedly, "but other birds of passage interest me."

"Me too. But they are difficult to see. Shall I describe one to you?"

"That might be a wise thing to do."

"Let us sit down."

She indicated a fallen pine which lay like a classroom form just off the path, and spread out her rumpled skirt with such care it might have been a ball-dress. Karlheinz was seized with rage. Had he not seen her a bare ten minutes before, half-naked, shameless? Now she sat, head bowed, almost virginal. What did she take him for?

"First," she demanded, "your credentials."

Karlheinz repeated what he had come prepared to say. She questioned him, skilfully, quickly, and leaned back, satisfied.

"You know why I am here?" There was a sudden formality about her.

"I know why you are supposed to be."

"It is good that they send you. It shows the value that is placed on a certain high-ranking officer in East Germany who is anxious for a change of air."

"If that were all he wanted I'm sure you could have arranged for it quite simply. You have very varied scenery."

"He has a hankering to see the Rhine and certain of your cities. Bonn, for instance, interests him very much."

"Please convey to him that the interest is mutual and I hope he will have a good journey and arrive in Bonn in health."

"He anticipates no problems, even with the frontier formalities."

"I am glad to hear it. And his health?"

"Excellent at present."

"Tell him to take great care of it. An attack of laryngitis, let us say, in our climate could prove fatal."

"He would find such an illness most distressing. He is a very sociable man."

"Easy to talk to?"

"Most forthcoming—in the right circles. And when he has something to say."

"Excellent. He would find the atmosphere in Bonn congenial."

"He would like to find himself among his own kind."

"High-ranking army officers—"

"—fond of discussing military strategy and dispositions. Perhaps even a ballistics expert or two."

"The modern army is a series of specialist branches. That shouldn't be difficult to arrange."

"I'm glad we understand each other so well, Herr Oberst."

"I did not doubt but that we should."

"Yet I think you found me a little disconcerting. Confess: I was not quite the emissary you had anticipated."

"No, I was agreeably surprised."

She laughed—a chiming of bells. "How charmingly you put it."

"The subject provokes the compliment."

She smiled—a warmth softer than sunlight suffused him for a second. "It is good when pleasure and business mix."

He laid a hand on her knee. She neither responded nor rebuffed him. She had warm blood but her skin was firm and cool.

"I shall report back," he told her.

"How long before you have an answer?"

"A few days. A week at most."

"Then why don't we meet again—here."

He was delighted and startled. "But the risk—for you, I mean!"

"Risks are a part of our profession."

"In the West we are taught not to take them needlessly."

"In that you show yourselves our inferiors."

"I think not. We have a greater regard for individual lives."

"All men are expendable, Herr Oberst."

"All?"

"Oh, yes. Unique but expendable."

Involuntarily Karlheinz took his hand from her knee.

"Now I've offended you," she said lightly. "But you will forgive me, won't you? Please!"

"Since we are to meet again I shall have to." Karlheinz had recovered from the momentary distaste with which the expression in her cold blue eyes had filled him. He replaced his hand and even moved it a little higher. She leaned towards him. Her breath was very sweet.

"Do you know the Harz?" she asked idly.

"As a boy I spent much time here with my aunts. Before the war."

"So you know our side of the frontier also?"

"As well as I know my own. And you — do you know the Harz?"

"I have visited here, but I am not a native."

"Where do you come from?"

"Somewhere very far away."

"East Prussia? Masuria?" he hazarded.

"Does it matter where one is born? — or where one dies?"

Karlheinz affected not to hear her. "Would I be right in thinking that the high-ranking officer we spoke of was born near Düsseldorf?"

"I thought we had agreed that the place did not matter, but yes, his papers say Düsseldorf."

Karlheinz was conscious of an inward jubilation. It could only be Liebermann to whom their conversation referred, the East's foremost guided weapons expert. He had been almost sure of it before, but that last long shot clinched it: Western files had no record of any other man of similar qualifications who was born near Düsseldorf. He was suddenly anxious to get away, to communicate with General Lohinsky where he sat at the centre of his web in Bonn. Gently he drew away from his companion.

"I must go — and I don't even know your name."

"You may call me Anna."

"You may call me Karl."

He was conscious of a twinge of uneasiness. Was it a little too near the truth? But there were doubtless East German files on him already; and the girl, after all, was working for the Western side.

They were on their feet now, facing each other. He leaned forward to kiss her lips.

"Till a week today then, Anna."

She drew him towards her with arms unexpectedly strong. The fervour of her response first startled, then pleased him. It was as though his soul were being drawn out of him. He heard himself panting slightly, felt her body yielding against his.

Then they were apart. She had drawn away when he knew he should have been the one to do so. As always, she seemed to have the upper hand. Her eyes regarded him with coolness, not with passion. He was reminded of how they had looked when he had first seen her, lying under the peasant in the grass.

"Dear Karl, you are impetuous for one so experienced."

The hint of mockery in her smile had spread to her voice.

"Tell your chief — what is his name? — "

"Lohinsky."

" — Tell Lohinsky from me when you next see him that he has picked exactly the right man for this job."

She laughed, and again he heard silver bells chiming, and watched her walk lightly, gracefully away. Where the path turned she looked back to wave, and seemed to vanish. He hurried to the corner but there was no sign of her on the pathway or in the woodland. It was as though she had never been.

It was only as he walked away that the full enormity of his action struck him. He had revealed the name of his chief, a man so carefully concealed that his existence was unsuspected by many of his own agents. And he, Ackermann, had given the name just like that.

He must have been out of his mind to cast aside years of training, of dissimulating until the false became the true. A schoolboy playing at spies would not have made such a blunder. He deserved to be stood against a wall and shot. As in a sense he might be. He had no illusions about the fate that was in store. He was honour bound to confess the extent of his betrayal. His career as an agent was at an end. And he knew too much to remain at liberty, especially once he was known to have a loose tongue. He shuddered, recalling a case some years ago when an ex-agent had met with a distressing accident. Or that was how his death had been described.

There was suicide, of course, the officer's honourable way out with a pistol. Perhaps on the whole that might be best. He would make his report, receive his new instructions as though nothing had happened, and then send Lohinsky a note. . . . But then he would not be able to keep next week's appointment. Would not a change of agent arouse suspicion on the other side? Was it not his duty to salvage what he could from this disaster and serve his country for as long as he might conceivably be of use? If Anna thought him such a fool — he writhed, remembering her mocking eyes — might she not relax her own guard a little? While she thought she was twisting him round her little finger, might he not be able to manipulate her? The idea appealed to him, her body was so pliant. He could imagine how it would feel beneath him on the ground.

He was approaching the field where he had surprised her with the peasant when he saw to his annoyance that the man was still there, lying face downwards in the grass almost as though he still had Anna beneath him. Karlheinz deliberately trod on a dead branch which snapped loudly, but the man did not look up as he drew near.

Something about his attitude seemed suddenly sinister and familiar. Karlheinz called out, but the fellow did not appear to hear. Certain now that he was dealing with a dead man, Karlheinz approached warily, anxious not to become involved in the inevitable police enquiries, and touched him. The body sank sideways, revealing a large patch of grass scarlet and sticky with blood. More blood welled from the mouthlike wound above his collar, where his throat had been cut from ear to ear.

The murder of the peasant, Bauer, was a sensation. Nothing like it had happened in the little town before. Bauer was a married man with five children, inclined to drink but no more of a womanizer than most. On the day in question he had taken his lunch with him and set off to work on the hill field, a strip of pasture well beyond the reach of any tractor, even if he had possessed such a thing. What woman had he met and presumably raped in such surroundings? What tigress was she to have retaliated so? What cool head had disposed so completely of bloodstained clothing and the murder weapon? The chief of police came to call upon Karlheinz.

"Forgive the intrusion, Herr Oberst. It's just that—well, you did inform us that you were in the woods that afternoon but saw and heard nothing. . . ."

"That is correct," Karlheinz said formally.

"Of course it is. No one doubts that, Herr Oberst, and we very much appreciate your help. You came forward, if I may say so, as one would have expected of you. Only, you know, people do sometimes forget. A significant fact escapes them, perhaps because they haven't realized its significance. So if we could just run through your statement again. . . ."

"Certainly," Karlheinz said, "if you wish."

He rapidly went over it in his own mind, as he answered preliminary questions. No, he had remembered everything. No mention of Anna—that was the most important. Everything else must be arranged round that. Even his route had had to be subtly altered, to take him well away from the scene of the crime. . . .

"And you saw nothing, no one, Herr Oberst?"

The police chief plodded doggedly on.

"Yes," Karlheinz said suddenly. "I saw one thing."

The police chief froze. "What was that?"

Karlheinz smiled in apology. "No help to you, I'm afraid. I saw a hare."

"A hare?"

Karlheinz's smile broadened. "Yes, the largest hare I've ever seen. Made me lick my lips, it was so meaty-looking. That's why I remember it."

"Pity you didn't have a gun," the chief of police said sadly. He too enjoyed roast hare.

"One doesn't walk about the peaceful Harz armed."

"You call them peaceful?" The police chief, diverted for a moment, shook his head. "Once, yes; one of the most idyllic regions of Germany. But now, with that accursed so-called frontier running through. . . . Ah no, Herr Oberst, they are only superficially peaceful. For us, they are a living reminder of the war."

"You needn't tell me," Karlheinz said. "I remember."

"Of course. I forget you are almost a native here."

"More than you are."

"I come from Hanover."

Karlheinz filed away the information. It might be useful later on. He said pointedly: "I hope you manage to clear this business up soon. The locals will expect it of you."

The police chief almost groaned. "Don't I know it! But every woman seems to be accounted for."

"One thing at least makes your job easier."

The police chief looked up. "What is that?"

Karlheinz red-herringed him skilfully. "The woman must have come from this side of the border. From this town, or else a neighbouring village. In the old days, you would have had to cast your net much farther afield."

"Which makes it all the worse if I don't succeed in making an arrest."

"The woman must be somewhere," Karlheinz argued. He would dearly have loved to know where.

The police chief said thoughtfully: "That is, if it *was* a woman. . . ."

Karlheinz leaned forward. "What do you mean?"

The police chief looked at the man before him. Plump, sleek, an army colonel on leave, a bachelor. The idea was not impossible. . . .

"We know," he said patiently, "that Bauer had had sexual intercourse shortly before he died. We have naturally assumed it was with a woman. What if we are wrong?"

"Was Bauer a homosexual?"

"There is no suggestion that he was."

"Well, then. . . ."

"What if he were offered money, Herr Oberst? Let us say a substantial sum."

Karlheinz did not care for the way the police chief was looking at him.

"Would the fellow be likely to accept?"

"I can't say. But Bauer was a primitive type, unlikely to raise objections. I think on the whole he would."

"That widens your field."

"Yes," the police chief said thoughtfully. "I must make enquiries what men were seen in the woods."

"I've already told you I saw no one."

"But you admit to being there yourself."

"I came forward in response to your appeal, you remember."

"Of course. If only someone else had done so as well. Then you could vouch for each other."

"Are you suggesting I might have slit that peasant's throat?"

"Indeed, no, Herr Oberst. No more than anyone else. But you must surely see that all who are known to have been in the woods are suspect."

Karlheinz was angry now. "You are implying that I might be guilty of unnatural practices and murder." God, if this fellow only knew!

"Only because you were in the woods, Herr Oberst, and someone in those woods killed Franz Bauer."

Karlheinz stood up. "I have nothing more to say to you."

The police chief also rose. "Then I need not trouble you any more. I am most grateful for your help, Herr Oberst." Karlheinz did not escort him to the door.

The days before he saw Anna passed in a fever. The police did not trouble him again. But neither did they make an arrest. The town was humming. The Widow Bauer was loud in her complaints.

"They'd have arrested someone fast enough if it was one of the town bigwigs had been murdered. If you ask me the police are afraid. They know who done it right enough and they're scared to touch her. Or else they're scared to touch *him*."

In this she did the police an injustice, and in any case no one took much notice of the Widow Bauer. Like her late husband, she was stupid to the point of being simple. All the same, it was too bad for murdering him like that.

Karlheinz set off for his next appointment with Anna aware of the suspicious looks that followed him. He had thought it wise to make no secret of where he was going. With equal candour, the citizens had let him know that they thought this was carrying curiosity or coincidence too far.

In other circumstances Karlheinz would have agreed with them and left the woods well alone. But there was his mission to consider. And there was Anna. He wanted to see her again.

Nevertheless, he was uneasy as he set off for his appointment, followed by unseen, unfriendly eyes. Was he also being followed more positively? He tried out several well-known tests. All proved negative. Reassured, he continued, confident that the police chief's minions were not a match for him. Had he not been trained by the Abwehr, who regarded him as one of their top agents? He pushed to the back of his mind the nagging question: did they still?

He would have been even more worried had he known that in Bonn General Lohinsky was looking at a confidential report made on the basis of local police enquiries about a certain Colonel Ackermann — enquiries which had been sidetracked skilfully.

"He hasn't been there a week and he goes and gets himself mixed up in some sordid local murder," Lohinsky complained. "Gets himself suspected, too. Oh, there's nothing in it. I know Ackermann and this doesn't bear his trademark. All the same, he's not the agent he used to be. As for this high-ranking defector he babbles about, well, we can only wait and see."

Fortunately for Karlheinz, he knew nothing of this conversation, and in any case his mind was soon distracted by the hare. He could not be positive that it was the same hare he had noticed on his first visit, but it seemed unlikely that there could be two that size. This time it sat up on the path ahead of him without the least sign of fear. It allowed him to approach until he could see its soft nose twitching. Then, with a flirtatious flick of its rump, it loped off. Once again he was struck by the effortless speed of its movement, by the gleam of almost human intelligence in its eye. Hares screamed like a woman, if wounded. He could understand why peasant superstition credited them with supernatural powers.

Karlheinz had been waiting some time before he saw Anna. Once again, it seemed to him, she just appeared. One minute the path was bare, the next she was walking towards him. She gave him her cheek to kiss.

When he tried to take her lips, she turned aside, laughing. "We have business to discuss. After, perhaps."

"You're late," he said.

"I had difficulty in getting here. There are many policemen in the woods today."

"Not on your side," he objected.

"I take a roundabout route. What is going on, Karl? Have you been careless? I do not like it when there are many people about."

Briefly he told her of the murder.

"It was hard," she said, "but it had to be done."

Although he knew she must have committed it, Karlheinz still experienced a shock, until he remembered those ice-cold eyes that had looked up at him from under the peasant's red and angry face.

He said stupidly: "Why did you do it?"

"He caught me as I was changing. I had to silence him."

"Changing?"

Anna was impatient. "You don't think I cross the frontier in these clothes?"

She indicated her dirndl dress. There was no doubt it suited her, with its full skirt that emphasized her slim waist and its bodice that pushed her breasts high. He wondered momentarily what disguise she used and where she had left it hidden. Whatever it was, it was a pretty effective one. And one whose secret was sufficiently vital for her to kill to preserve it. He imagined Bauer coming upon the girl half-naked. It would have been provocation for any man.

"What weapon did you use?" he asked idly.

"My own, of course. I carry a knife."

Karlheinz wondered if she said it as a warning. But after all, he also carried a knife.

Anna had seated herself on the log and was patting the place beside her. "To business," she said. She made it sound like an invitation to anything but.

Karlheinz sat down beside her, put his arm round her, and allowed his fingers to stray towards her breast. In such circumstances the movement was so familiar to him that he was surprised he even noticed it, until he realized that it proceeded not from any desire on his part, but from a definite and conscious one on hers. I ought to leave her alone, he told himself, but it was as though her flesh exerted a magnetic pull on his. In an effort to keep control of the situation, he said more brusquely than he intended:

"Well, what news of Liebermann?"

Anna drew away from him, offended. "I am not aware that we have mentioned names."

"No, but that's who it is, isn't it? It must be. He's your only important ballistics expert and he was born in Düsseldorf. Don't tell me he wasn't, for I checked."

"Dear Karl." Her words caressed him. "You are so thorough. And if I may say so, such a fool. You are so excited at having, as you think, identified our would-be defector, that you are in danger of being arrested for murder. The police suspect you, you know."

"What do you know about it?"

"I have heard various things."

"There are no witnesses."

"No," Anna said thoughtfully, "but witnesses might be produced. It would be easy to supply one who could give circumstantial details but who had been afraid to come forward till now."

Karlheinz felt himself grow cold. "What are you hinting at?"

"I'm only trying to warn you, my dear." She laughed and silver bells rang in his head. "No, I assure you—you've nothing to fear from me. I'm on your side. I'm not trying to turn you into a double agent. I just want you to appreciate—facts."

"Such as?"

"Such as that it is difficult for General Liebermann—or his go-between—to have confidence in an opposite number about whom so little is known."

"You know perfectly well our work doesn't call for the production of credentials beyond those I gave you last time."

She looked up at him. "The swallows are late again this year," she quoted softly.

"Exactly." Her lips were so near that he kissed them without intending to. He felt her arms go round him. Her dress was slipping from her shoulder. Beneath him, he felt the quiver of her laugh.

"You take yourself so seriously," she panted. "I cannot resist teasing you. Next week, when I come, I shall have someone with me. To make sure you behave yourself."

"A chaperone?"

"It will be a new rôle for him."

"You mean *you're* going to bring Liebermann—here?"

"Why not?"

"But—"

"The mechanics of it are my business. All you have to do is to inform Lohinsky in—where is it? Bonn?"

"No. 19, Kalverstrasse."

"I know. I meant the covering address."

"The Rhineland Insurance Company, Limited."

"Then please tell the Rhineland Insurance Company to be prepared to take delivery of an important consignment of goods from East Germany, to be forwarded via their agent Karlheinz Ackermann. No, don't be startled. Of course I know your name."

"Don't you know mine?" she added a moment later.

Karlheinz was too busy to reply. His urgent flesh was hot and so was Anna's, though if he had looked he would have seen that her eyes were cold.

This time when she left him he followed her discreetly to where there was a bend in the path. By the time he reached it, she had vanished. She must have turned aside, but no broken bush betrayed her passage. In the silence of the woods he had heard no snapping twig. The path did not branch. There was nowhere she could have gone to, unless she had been transformed into a tree: one of those slim birches whose leaves were shaken by the wind as if by laughter. It was only what he would have expected from such a witch.

For she had bewitched him. There was no other explanation. No woman had ever before affected him like this. He had taken and used and cast them aside like empty vessels, and thinking back, he could not even tell them apart. But Anna was different if only because of the contrast between her hot lips and the cool intensity of her gaze, between her pliant body and implacable will, between her lucid intelligence and her animal sensuality. The scent of her still lingered in his nostrils, his fingers tingled with her touch. He buried his face in his hands and groaned her name until the pine-trees took it up and the wind whispered it among their branches. And the wind's spicy, pine-laden breath came back to him like a sigh of love.

He knew very well what he should do was to return to his hotel, take out the pistol hidden in the false bottom of his bag, and blow his brains out, leaving no note, no explanation, and allowing the world to draw what conclusions it would. The chief of police would doubtless treat it as an admission of guilt and consider the Bauer case closed. Lohinsky would regard it as the failure of a mission and a solution convenient to all concerned. Anna would—what would Anna make of it? She could not despise him more than she did, this agent who had allowed her to run rings round him and then, conscience-stricken, had taken the easy, so-called honourable way out.

The enormity of his guilt could not be denied for a moment. He had blown the whole operation, cover and names and all, answering Anna's artless questions as if he were a schoolboy coming up with the right answers in class. Anna would never entrust him with Liebermann. In her circle he must be a laughing-stock. He did not believe her promise to conduct Liebermann to him by the same mysterious route she used herself. She had tested him deliberately and found him wanting because he, Ackermann the unassailable, had sold himself, his network, his country, for her body taken on a pine-needle bed.

But what a body! Even now its perfection charmed him, and its imperfections charmed him even more. Such as the little raised mole under her armpit, like a third nipple nestling there. He had whispered, biting it gently: "In the Middle Ages they would have burned you as a witch." "I *am* a witch," Anna had murmured, twisting her fingers in his hair.

Now, looking back, he could scarcely believe any of it had happened. It had never been like that before. His fingers strayed with satisfaction to the row of blue marks near the base of his throat, where Anna had bitten him. "I could bite your throat out," she had laughed.

He wondered for an instant briefer than lightning if that was how the peasant had died, but no; that had been a knife wound; he had seen it and there was no mistaking it. It was some time later that he made the discovery that his own knife had gone.

He noticed the torn lining protruding from his sleeve, and then realized that the knife it concealed had vanished. Of course he might easily have torn it in his exertions; even so, the knife should not have fallen out. He explored gently and found that the strap holding it had been unfastened, as if deliberately. The obvious suspect was Anna, but what did she want with his knife? She had already proved that she had one of her own and knew how to use it. No, his love-making must have jerked the fastening loose.

Still, it was one more thing not to mention to Lohinsky in what had become by now a carefully edited report. And Lohinsky, tossing it aside, muttered angrily:

"Whether he delivers Liebermann or not, Ackermann has outlived his usefulness. We shall have to dispose of him."

On the way to his third appointment with Anna, Karlheinz looked out for the hare. It had become a kind of good luck symbol which gave him confidence to go on.

Sure enough, round a bend in the path it was waiting for him. Its attitude suggested exactly that. It was sitting up, ears cocked, forepaws hanging limply, with its bright eyes fixed on his approach. Once again, it allowed him to come within a few yards before retreating, but this time it did not retreat very far. It took a few graceful bounds up the hillside, and then sat up and concentrated on him again. Karlheinz waved to it and it dipped one ear in acknowledgment. Then, flirting its rump again, it loped away. He wondered how long before its fearlessness was its undoing. Someone would certainly shoot the creature one day.

The early June weather was perfect. The sun shone from an almost cloudless sky. The woodland rang with birdsong. The spicy pine scent hung heavily in the air. Somewhere a woodpecker rat-tatted. A squirrel chattered overhead. The surrounding hills blurred blue towards a heat-hazy horizon. The Brocken rose majestically over all.

Karlheinz noted that its summit was now bare of whiteness. The witches had swept the last of the snow away. This too seemed to him a happy omen. For once everything was going as it should.

In his exalted state he almost forgot the explaining he would sooner or later have to do. Lohinsky would not take kindly to learning that his organization's cover was blown and he himself identified. He would certainly never understand. Indeed, Karlheinz himself did not understand it. How could an experienced agent do such a thing? Especially one notoriously immune to women's blandishments. He almost wondered if he had been drugged. It would certainly be the easiest explanation, except that it was impossible. He had accepted nothing from Anna but her body, and she could scarcely drug him with that. He had even examined himself for punctures in case she had injected him unawares, but as he expected, there was nothing. He had no defence. He had simply been a fool. And reluctantly he recognized that the price of folly was likely to be a high one. His career was finished, even if he successfully delivered Liebermann; if he did not, his life might well be forfeit too.

In that peaceful, sunlit silence the sound of the explosion was so shocking that Karlheinz almost jumped out of his skin. It was followed by an instant's complete stillness, and then by a long scream of human agony whose echoes seemed to persist indefinitely. There was only one thought in Karlheinz's head, and that was Anna. This time she had failed to get through. Her incredible luck had at last deserted her. The mines had got her in the end. Almost at once a machine-gun fired a burst and then another. It was somewhere very close at hand. Not wanting to see, yet unable to resist the impulse, Karlheinz began to run towards the nearest look-out point.

He ran clumsily, like a man uncertain where he is going. Twice he slipped, and once he almost fell. He heard the sounds of his progress, heard himself gasping and cursing, as much at his own helplessness as at the trees and scrub that barred his path. It seemed that he would never reach the natural bastion that commanded a view of the demarcation zone.

In happier days it had simply been a viewpoint, from which cheerful knickerbocker-clad hikers could admire the view. Now its rôle was more sinister. The view was still there for those who cared to look at it, but attention was concentrated now on the broad band of felled tree-stumps, bracken and saplings, that ran through the heart of Germany. Karlheinz was no exception. His eyes went at once to what they sought: a huddle of bloodstained clothing at the foot of the farther slope among the bracken. He could not distinguish anything else.

Then voices rang out, excited, angry. An officer shouted orders. Two stretcher-bearers emerged. Gingerly, with the officer leading, the three men began to pick their way from the East German side. Karlheinz could see the unfamiliar uniform quite clearly. They were following a devious route, no doubt the secret path across the minefield that Anna must so often have used.

The bloodstained heap never moved. Karlheinz had no hope that it was living, but he stayed none the less. It was the last tribute he could pay to someone brave and beautiful and beloved. Even when the soldiers reached the heap and the officer kicked it, he could not turn his eyes away.

The stretcher-bearers bent down, and when they straightened he saw that their hands were red. He felt sickness gathering in his throat as they stooped again and this time lifted the sagging, ungainly burden. He saw a trailing arm, a leg bent at an unnatural angle; he could not distinguish a head.

But what he could distinguish, quite unmistakably, was that the body was that of a man. It was a tall man. It was not Anna. It must have been Liebermann.

In his agitation he had forgotten that Liebermann was coming. He was the one who had trodden on the mine. Less skilful, less experienced than Anna, he had been unable to follow her and get through. Which meant that Anna might already be waiting for him, wondering why he failed to keep the rendezvous.

She was not there. Karlheinz was so disappointed he would have liked to burst into tears, as he had done in childhood when told, "Your mother's coming," and his mother had failed to turn up. It was a moment or two before the other possibility occurred to him: that Anna might have been taken prisoner by the other side, leaving the helpless Liebermann to flounder unaided through the minefield, with predictable and horrible results. But not more horrible than what would be done to Anna if she were caught red-handed helping a defector to escape. She was not here, so that was the only possible explanation. They would go to work on her at once. Bit by bit they would drag everything she knew out of her: the secret path through the minefield, her contact on the other side, Lohinsky's name, the Rhineland Insurance cover. . . . That body which had so delighted him would be broken and twisted, the mole under her armpit the subject of some coarse jest. And there was nothing he or anyone could do to help this girl whom he knew only as Anna. Karlheinz sat down on the log where he had sat beside her and bowed his head so that the forest should not see he wept.

The snapping of a twig aroused him. Someone was coming. Several people. They were trampling through the wood like wild boars. Karlheinz stood up, instinctively aware that he was their quarry, but quite unprepared to see the chief of police appear.

The men with him fanned out into a semicircle.

"I suppose you know what's happened?" Karlheinz said.

"We know the full story now, Ackermann." The police chief's voice was unexpectedly harsh. Gone was the deferential "Herr Oberst," or even the "Herr" which courtesy required. He was being addressed like a felon, but Karlheinz was too distraught to care.

"They've got her, they must have done, a mine exploded and then their machine-guns opened up. . . ."

"We heard." The police chief's voice was still cold, still unrelenting. "But it's none of our business. We're instructed to take no notice of these incidents unless someone actually gets across."

"But she did. Several times. It's only today that—"

"Karlheinz Ackermann." The police chief sounded even more hostile. "I must formally caution you that anything you say may be used in evidence against you, and I arrest you on the charge of murdering Franz Bauer."

The peasant! Karlheinz looked at him stupidly.

"I never touched the man."

The police chief nodded to two of his officers, who stepped forward and pinioned Karlheinz's arms to his sides.

He looked at them helplessly. "I didn't do it. There must be some mistake."

"We have a witness," the police chief said implacably.

"But there wasn't a soul about."

"No one you saw, perhaps, but this young woman from a neighbouring village, who has been afraid to come forward till now, says that she saw you coming away from the body and cleaning your knife on the grass."

"My knife—"

"Perhaps you can produce it."

"No," Karlheinz said. "I can't. I lost it. But that was after the murder. . . ."

His mind was beginning to spin. Anna had taken his knife. Anna had framed him. But why, when she was on his side? Then doubts poured in. Lohinsky had always suspected her. That was why the mission had been assigned to him—an agent whom they were not averse to losing. Anna had betrayed him and they would not lift a finger to help.

"Your knife was found," the police chief was saying, "where you thought you had hidden it. It has been forensically tested and there are traces of Bauer's blood still on it, although it has been recently cleaned."

"I didn't kill him," Karlheinz said stupidly.

Anna had killed him. She had admitted as much. But no one would have heard of Anna. They would think he had invented her. Lohinsky was the only person, and Lohinsky had said at the outset, "You're in this on your own." He had no alibi—he had admitted being in the woods—and now Anna had produced a false witness, as she had said all along she might. She had taken his knife. She had transferred some of Bauer's blood to it, from her stained clothing or from the blood-soaked grass. She had lured him again to the woods and had the police tipped off regarding his whereabouts. She had deliberately led Liebermann into a trap.

He was no longer surprised that Anna was not there to meet him, nor fearful of what they were doing to her on the other side. They were fêting her, toasting her, calling her the greatest of their agents. They knew every detail of her mysterious goings to and fro.

The police chief jerked his head sharply, and the two officers tightened their grip on Karlheinz.

"Come on, march."

They were not unfriendly, merely doing their duty, but how he hated them. Another man stepped forward, there was a clink of metal and the click of a lock snapping home. Karlheinz looked down in horror at the handcuffs, and protest rose to his lips.

"Keep the explanations for your lawyer," the police chief commanded. "You'll have some explaining to do."

He gave his orders. Someone shoved Karlheinz in the small of the back, his manacled hands were jerked forward. Awkwardly the little procession moved off, the police chief bringing up the rear, swinging his revolver. Karlheinz kept his head down.

It was the one good thing he did, he was to think later. If he had not, he would not have seen the hare, which came bounding down the slope towards them as if in slow motion, and stopped a few yards from the path. There it sat up, nose twitching. He was irresistibly reminded of Anna's nose. It drooped an ear as if in mocking salutation, turned, flicking its tail contemptuously, and loped nonchalantly away.

"For God's sake, shoot that damned hare!"

Karlheinz heard his voice come raspingly. The sight of this former symbol of good fortune was more than he could bear.

Either from sympathy, or perhaps because he liked roast hare, and thought the opportunity too good to miss, the police chief fired his revolver. The hare sprang vertically upwards, uttered a long thin wailing scream like a woman's, half fell, righted itself, and made off draggingly, leaving a trail of blood.

The police chief fired again, several of his men drew their weapons, but the wounded hare had reached thick undergrowth.

"Let it alone," the police chief ordered. "We didn't come here to go hunting." He clapped Karlheinz bravely on the shoulder. "Or rather, we've got what we came out to get."

In a room in East Germany a few days later two men were entering some details on a card. The card bore the code name "Anna." When he had finished, one of the men ruled a thick black line across it and looked up.

"Nothing I hate more than writing 'finis' to a good agent, especially when I don't know how she died."

"I thought she was shot trying to cross the border from West Germany."

The other man said, "It wasn't quite like that."

Anna had just completed a successful mission. Not only had she learned important details of their organization from the fool they had sent to meet her from the West, but she had been instrumental in framing him on a murder charge in his own country, which the prosecution would undoubtedly be able to prove. Moreover, she had succeeded in unmasking one of their own would-be defectors and seeing to it that he met an unpleasant end among the minefields and machine-guns on the frontier, thereby saving the state much trouble and expense.

"If she was so successful, how come she didn't make it?"

His companion said: "That we shall never know. She was found dying from loss of blood and bullet wounds on our side of the border. None of our guards saw her coming—they say they never did. She died without speaking and we shall never know who shot her. But someone used a revolver on her."

"A revolver! But that means close quarters."

"Perhaps she was careless. Even good agents sometimes are. But I wish we knew the secret of how she went to and fro at will across the border. We could make good use of it."

"Do you think anyone else could follow in her footsteps?"

"No. She was exceptional in every way. She could charm any man into doing what she wanted, with her beauty, her laugh like silver bells chiming, that fascinating mole under her armpit—" The head of the organization stopped short.

His subordinate, who had long suspected that Anna was his mistress, said, smiling, "You make her sound like a witch."

DAVY JONES'S TALE

THE GUIDING LIGHT, A BARQUENTINE OF THREE HUNDRED TONS homeward bound from America, was shipwrecked off the coast of Pembrokeshire one hundred years ago, with the loss of all hands — for the lone survivor who was washed ashore next morning was raving and did not live more than a few weeks.

It is necessary that you should know this because without it nothing in this tale makes sense. There are those who say — though I am not of them — that it makes no sense even with it, but of that you must be the judge.

I was born David Matthew Jones in Porthfynnon, a village on the north coast of Pembrokeshire, in April 1945. My father, David Jones, had gone down with his ship when she was torpedoed a bare six months before. My mother used to say that the night he died he came back and stood within our cottage doorway, looking at her a long time and sadly shaking his head. But she was a woman, and fanciful. She died when I was eight.

Thereafter I was brought up by my uncle, Robert Jenkins, and his son Owen was like a brother to me, except that, two years older than I, he was tall and ruddy, whereas I am dark and slight. He could do everything in this world better than I could, except for swimming and making love. For the swimming, anyone in the village will tell you that Davy Jones is own brother to a fish. And for the love-making, I have Agnes's word on it, and that is good enough for me.

But in the time before Agnes, Owen and I were inseparable, and no sweetness in the love of woman can equal that in the companionship of men. What one did, the other did also. We fought often, and nearly always Owen beat me, but he would fight for me if need be. And as I grew older and better able to hold my own and no longer needed his protection, I fought his battles too, and he was glad of me.

But there were differences. When Owen left school he joined his father in his fishing-boat, but when I left school the master sent for me.

"Davy," he said, "you are down to leave us in the summer. What are you going to do?"

"Why, Mr. Lloyd," I said, "I'm going in the boat with my uncle and Owen."

"So you want to be a fisherman, hey?"

I spread my hands. "My father was a fisherman. I was born to it, as you might say."

"An honourable calling," Mr. Lloyd said. "St. Peter was a fisherman. But that's two thousand years ago. A more sophisticated age has more sophisticated opportunities. Have you never thought of staying on at school?"

"I'm sorry, sir, but I think school's a waste of time."

He coloured a little. "That sounds as if we've failed you."

"No, no," I said, "you got me through the school-leaving exam."

"But, Davy, there are other exams you could take, technical qualifications you could try for."

"Will they teach me to handle a boat better than I do?"

"Probably not. But how much longer will your boat go on putting out? Economic conditions are against you. The small boat-owner's day is done."

"We may have unemployment in Milford Haven, but we still manage to get the catch away."

"But can you go on doing so? The railways are threatening closure. It's like the ports in the last century—too small to develop, not big enough to be economic as they were. There's no living to be made from the sea off Pembrokeshire."

"A man can still drown in it, though."

Mr. Lloyd thought it an odd remark, and said so, but to me it was the most natural in the world. Too many of our secluded bays are ripped by cruel currents. When the wind's in the south-west, you can hear the surf far inland. For as long as I could remember, Uncle Robert, like his father and grandfather, had gone out with the lifeboat whenever there was a ship in distress. It happens surprisingly often in our waters. Now Owen too had joined the lifeboat's crew.

It was thinking of this that made me speak of drowning—that and the long row of graves in the churchyard, many being anonymous sailors washed up along the coast around Porthfynnon, but the majority belonging to the crew of *The Guiding Light*.

I told Mr. Lloyd so, but he saw little relevance in the fate of a vessel lost so many years before, and concentrated on trying to get me to go on with the schooling, which I was set against. It is hard now to say why, but it had something to do with independence. I wanted to rank with the men rather than the boys; to earn my own living even if it was not a fat one; above all, to be with Uncle Robert and Owen in their boat. These last two years I had wakened night after night and lain there biting my pillow to hear them creep downstairs in the dark and make ready to be off with the tide, while I, hours later, came down to Aunt Miriam scolding over breakfast and had to be away to school. Then, one afternoon, perhaps days later, I would return to find them feasting like heroes, the catch entrained and their oilskins and sea-boots hanging once again behind the door. It is small wonder that I wanted to be done with schooling. Only old Lloyd would have tried to get me to stay.

Mind you, once or twice since I have wondered if he was maybe less of a fool than I thought him, for it is right enough that the fishing has grown very bad. Several men in Porthfynnon have laid up their boats, and I knew — none better — that the living would never be a fat one, but we had luck and we managed to make ends meet. So I was the more surprised when one day Owen, while he was taking a turn at the wheel, with me beside him and Uncle Robert catching up on sleep below, announced in a voice that seemed to me to carry unnaturally far over the quiet-breathing waters, "Davy, I am going away."

"Where to, then?" I asked, stupid.

"To Cardiff. Swansea, maybe. Where there's work and wages and a man isn't always scratching for a living." He added softly. "For I am sick of it here."

If he had uttered blasphemy I could not have been more shaken. To exchange our world of wind and sky and water for the hemmed-in noisiness of city streets; to breathe the stench of humanity and exhaust gases rather than the gorse and seaweed on our salt-laden, gull-loud air — these were things so alien to me that I felt a shock of horror, for I had assumed Owen felt the same.

Now he said matter-of-factly: "You'll go on giving Dad a hand with the boat. It's a better living for two and she works easy. And quiet Mam when she starts fretting herself. It's not the end of the world I'm going to, and I'll come home and see you all from time to time."

I nodded. I couldn't speak — it was as if Owen were dying. His next words made it worse: "Oh, and Davy, take my place in the lifeboat — Dad'll like to have you along."

Uncle Robert was coxswain now, and the *Margaret Freeling* was only less dear to him than his own boat. Although it was the motor mechanic's job to keep her at all times ready for launching, Uncle Robert went to check over her every week, and very often Owen and I went with him. I knew the lifeboat-station very well.

Although she is the Porthfynnon lifeboat, the *Margaret Freeling*'s launching station is more than a mile away, in a sheltered, westward-facing rocky inlet which is a natural harbour, with the lifeboat shed cliff-high and reached by a causeway, and the slipway a steep one-in-five gradient to the sea. There are not so many lifeboat-stations like

Porthfynnon, and ours is less than a hundred years old, for the boat used to put out from Porthfynnon harbour itself until they discovered its limitations. But that was after the disaster of *The Guiding Light*.

I have mentioned *The Guiding Light* several times already, so I had best take time to explain what is so special for Porthfynnon about this disaster, and why it has such a bearing on my tale.

Off the Pembrokeshire coast are many isolated rocks and islands that have broken away from the land. Those which rise above the tide are now the haunt of breeding sea-birds: eligugs—which is what we call guillemots—razorbills, shearwaters and puffins, and thousands upon thousands of gulls. But not all these rocks thrust up above the water; many are submerged even at low tide, yet near enough the surface to rip the plates of a ship's keel and hole her, and large enough to catch and hold her fast.

The Guiding Light was bound for Tenby—in 1870 Tenby was still an ocean-going port—but she was unlucky enough to run into an almighty storm, which blew her northwards and wrecked her on the Abbot and his Monks. This line of wicked rocks is less than a mile offshore just south of Porthfynnon. The Abbot is never quite submerged even at the highest tide, but his Monks are invisible even at neap tides; and in trying to avoid the Abbot, many a vessel has shipwrecked on his Monks. And *The Guiding Light,* though stoutly built, was a wooden vessel. In no time her planking was stove in, while great seas washed over her, sweeping her decks and pounding her to pieces. Within an hour her foremast had gone, snapped in two.

Fortunately it was still light and many people saw her. They raised the alarm and the lifeboat was pushed out. And then the horrid truth became apparent: the very winds and seas that had driven *The Guiding Light* onto the Monks and were battering her to pieces prevented the lifeboat from getting beyond the harbour mouth. And when she did so, by a superhuman effort, the men pulling at their oars until their sinews seemed about to break, the seas were so high that the coxswain, who was Uncle Robert's grandfather, my great-grandfather, realized he could never get near *The Guiding Light*. He ordered the lifeboat to put back to harbour. They would try again at first light. There were some who said he had given up too quickly, but it is not easy to see what else he could have done. He would only have added his crew to the bodies in the churchyard. Nevertheless, in Porthfynnon the argument about it sometimes still goes on.

I have heard Uncle Robert say that he remembers his grandfather explaining—he was everlastingly explaining—that at the time he thought the wreck would last the night. But for the next two hours the storm increased in violence, which would surely have put an end to the lifeboat. In the screaming wind, the rain, and the darkness, *The Guiding Light* broke up.

No one will ever know exactly what happened. With the first grey light it was apparent she was no longer there. Only planks of timber showed dark for a moment on the sea's heaving surface. And then the bodies began to come in. The wind had veered, and though strong, it was no longer at gale force; it was driving straight onto the land, and as the tide came in inert human figures were visible, rolling over and over in the surf. The sea brought twenty of them ashore and left them at high-water in a bay that we call the Bay of Seals, because in spring the Atlantic Grey Seals use it as a nursery. Now it was a mortuary. Many of the bodies were mutilated by the rocks. One of them was a woman. She had a young child in her arms. Her eyes were still open as if in grief or horror, and nothing the village women could do would get them closed. She was thought to be the captain's wife, but no one knew for certain; in those days passenger lists were not kept. She was buried with the rest in a plain deal coffin in our little churchyard, which is sheltered and flower-bright and out of the sound of the sea.

One man, when they found him, was still breathing, though he lay unconscious for days, and when he recovered his wits were wanting, so he could give no one any help. Since he was not violent and no one came forward to claim him, he stayed in the village and two weaving women looked after him. From the orders he sometimes shouted, making passers-by start like jumping-jacks, he was thought to have been the first or second mate. But he did not long survive his companions. In the short days around Christmas he died. With him went the last trace of *The Guiding Light,* and the tragedy would soon have been forgotten had it not been for the re-siting of the lifeboat shed.

Men from London came down and held an enquiry, and looked at all the coast around, and made recommendations and went back to London, and in due course their decision was announced. Soon after the new lifeboat-station was begun a mile to the north of Porthfynnon, with a slipway that carries it beyond the line of the surf. Uncle Robert used to say it was a fine position and the wreck of *The Guiding Light* had done some good at least, but Aunt Miriam would shake her head and murmur that the poor souls who perished in her might not think so. Uncle Robert pretended not to hear.

They took Owen's going very well after the first announcement, but the cottage was not the same. Aunt Miriam was forever watching for the postman, although Owen's letters were infrequent and never said much. He found a job in the docks in Cardiff, and came home once or twice, but when he did he was like a stranger. He talked of staying away indefinitely. Maybe it was this that lulled me, for I came to regard his absence as permanent. The boat was Uncle Robert's and mine, and I conveniently forgot about Owen, just as I forgot it was his place I had in the lifeboat's crew. So it fairly knocked me silly when, after three years, a letter came from him to say he was returning home for good and bringing with him the girl who would shortly be his bride. The night they were due, I drove into Haverfordwest to meet them and that is when I first saw Agnes. But that is another part of my tale.

I cannot say that Agnes was beautiful. If she had been, I should have been afraid of her and then none of this might have come about. It was sheeting with rain in Haverfordwest, and as I saw Owen come past the ticket-collector I thought of nothing but how good it was to see him again. I felt his hand in mine, strong and warm and vital, and heard the ring of his voice, and then he turned to the girl who stood silently beside him, and said, "Agnes, this is my cousin, Davy Jones."

I am not tall, so I did not have to look down on her; instead, her eyes were on a level with mine—grey eyes I thought them then, but later I learned better: Agnes's eyes were as many-hued and changing as the sea. Her voice too was low and murmuring, like waves that barely break on a summer's day. For the rest, I had an impression of rain glistening on a plastic mac and headscarf and running like tears down a round cheek.

Later, when I had a chance to see her in the cottage, I saw that everything about Agnes was round and full: her waist was too small, or her breasts and hips were too generous; her neck was too short, but the throat had the sweet firm whiteness of a nut. There are those who would have called her dumpy, and I cannot say that they would have been wrong; but even her detractors must have fallen silent at sight of the hair upon her head. Never have I seen such hair on a woman; she wore it piled high like a golden crown. When she let it down, as I discovered later, it rippled over her arms and shoulders as if she had undone a bale of silk.

I watched her all the time that first evening as though my life depended on it, and had not a word to say. I heard Owen's voice rise and fall as he talked about his plans and about the wedding, which was to be in Porthfynnon since Agnes was without near relatives, and for afterwards he would do up the old Davies cottage which was standing empty, and—"Davy, you'll be my best man?" I did not hear him, being too much occupied with looking at Agnes, and he had to say it again. I said yes without thinking, and there was much joking and laughter, and when I went to bed—early so as to be tactful—it seemed as if Agnes's laugh was still reechoing in my head.

Never having been in love before, I was slow to recognize the symptoms, but next day and all the day after there was a restlessness in my blood like the urge to wander, except that I was centred on Agnes, and all journeys from the cottage, even so short a one as to the harbour, were bearable only because they would end in the joy of coming back to her.

Perhaps I use this simile of the wanderlust because I became aware after a few days that it was expected of me that I should go away. Owen had spent his years in the wilderness and was come home with a fine bride as his portion: now it was the turn of Davy, untried, unwedded, to leave home and be out of Owen's way. Not that anything was said, but when Owen talked about Cardiff, I felt Aunt Miriam looking at me; when we returned from a fishing trip and the proceeds were divided, it was as though Uncle Robert wanted still to divide by two and not by three. Only Owen himself showed no signs of resentment.

"Why did you come back?" I said to him one day.

His reply shook me. "Because Agnes wanted it. She'd no love for the city and it was her suggestion we should come here. For myself, I liked it well enough away."

My sister-in-law-to-be was good at the weaving, and she had some education and a brain. It was her intention to start up a weaving community in Porthfynnon, where the skill had long languished, like those throughout Wales which now cater to the tourist trade. With that and the fishing she and Owen would make a living. Someday, Owen mused, he might even have his own boat. Meanwhile the wedding was only two weeks off, the ring already bought and entrusted to my safe-keeping, and still I lacked the courage to make myself up and go.

I remember nothing at all of that wedding except that my new shoes were too tight, and I stood beside Owen shifting from one foot to the other as though I were the one impatient for the bride to arrive. When she did, I could not look at her, and strangely, I had the feeling that she could not look at me. But I did not drop the ring. The minister blessed it and Owen put it on his bride's finger, and I cursed it because it would lie forever between my love and me.

After they returned from honeymoon, they moved into the old Davies cottage at the far end of the village and I saw little of Agnes — I supposed she was setting the cottage to rights. Aunt Miriam was often there keeping an eye on things — though she did not warm to Agnes — but Uncle Robert and I would not go uninvited. Owen often said, "You must come and see us, Davy." "When Agnes is ready," I would reply.

It was as though she were avoiding me. Often I would return from the fishing, clumping my way sea-booted up the street, in time to see Agnes slip out of our cottage and, not even pausing to turn and wave, set off almost at a run. And Aunt Miriam would say with grudging approval when questioned: "Yes, Agnes was here. She saw you coming and went home to get the kettle on for Owen. She thinks the world of him."

For Owen's sake I was glad, but Aunt Miriam's next words made me angry. "And now I suppose it'll be your turn to go gallivanting off to Cardiff and bringing some street girl back."

"How can you say such a thing of Agnes!"

"Ah, I've got eyes in my head."

"And a vile tongue in your mouth."

"Quick you are to defend her! Steer clear of her sort, Davy, when it comes time for you to go away."

"I am not thinking of going away," I told her.

"Oh." She hid her disappointment. "Well, you know what you're about, I dare say."

I did not tell her that I had no idea, that I lived out each day and fell asleep at the end of it wondering what point there was in my life. Twice I almost went to the minister, but I could not bring myself to tell him I desired my cousin's wife. "Whosoever looketh upon a woman to lust after her, that same hath committed adultery with her in his heart." How often had I heard it thundered forth on Sunday. In Porthfynnon, despite all you see on the television, we took the Ten Commandments seriously.

When we were not at sea, with the three of us—Uncle Robert, myself, and Owen—so close in the small boat that we could all but hear each other's thoughts, except that Owen could never have heard mine or he would have used his superior strength to throw me overboard, I took to going for long walks. Day after day I tramped along the cliff paths, past headlands blue with squill and pink with thrift; skirting clumps of sea-campion, heads bowed before the lightest breeze yet never breaking in a high wind, which lay among the rocks like drifts of springtime snow.

One day, when the air was warm with promise of summer and the short flowered turf alive with bees, I walked rather farther than I meant to, and came to the Bay of Seals. I was walking into the wind, and on the close grass my footsteps were silent. I had an excellent view of the nursery: grey cows, almost indistinguishable until they moved from the smooth rocks on which they were lying; the white, brown-spotted baby seals with their round, wide-open, human-seeming eyes; and out to sea, the old bulls standing sentinel, their whiskered noses raised suspiciously.

I stood there for some time, listening to the grunting, snorting, and barking, not very different from nurseries everywhere, until all at once the whole colony began slithering seawards, as though the rocks themselves were on the move. In a few seconds the Bay of Seals was empty, except for a crowd of round dark heads bobbing reproachfully offshore. I looked round to see what had startled them, and saw Agnes coming towards me over the turf.

Impulsively I held out my hands, and as impulsively she took them. For a moment we had no need of words. Nevertheless, I said, still holding her hands and guessing already at her answer: "Agnes, what brings you here?"

"I needed air," she said, as though Porthfynnon were a vacuum. "And also"—she lowered her eyes—"I saw you come this way."

My blood leapt but my brain stayed stagnant. "I thought you were avoiding me."

"I am. I have been." She was laughing, crying. "Oh, Davy, are you never going to go away?"

It was as though the sun went in. "Do you want me to?" I asked, still stupid.

"Don't you understand?" She broke from me. "Davy, I am Owen's wife and it is you I should have married, and now it is all too late. I have made my bed and must lie on it. But if there is to be any peace for me in Owen's arms, it can only be when you are absent. Davy, for my sake — because I love you and I should not — I am asking you to go away."

"Agnes — " I said. And tried again: "Agnes — " And the words stuck in my throat.

She had turned from me, her shoulders shaking. When I touched her, she flinched as though my hand were red-hot iron. I drew her to me, but she kept her head down and I loosened her hair and rocked her as if she were a child against me, murmuring more to myself than to her that I had not known, had never known, had never even suspected. . . .

"Don't!" she cried. "You're making it worse. I didn't know either. You were so aloof. You looked at me as if I wasn't there. And now night after night you torture me because it's you I respond to when Owen takes me in his arms."

"Is Owen no good, then?"

"I did not say that. But you would be better. I *know*." She looked up at me, her face still tear-stained. "There! Now I've shocked you — I can tell. I'm not the prim virgin you in Porthfynnon imagine. I told Owen — I don't cheat — and he was still ready to marry me, which is more than any of the others would have done."

"Was that why you wanted to leave Cardiff — because of your past?" I said, thinking Aunt Miriam's suspicions were well justified.

"My past!" She laughed bitterly, then pulled free and said as if reciting a lesson: "I am Mrs. Owen Jenkins, a respectable village matron, and that is how I intend to stay. And then, before I was even wedded, the Devil sent you to tempt me. Is there to be no peace, no respite, from the everlasting temptations of the flesh?"

"Only by yielding to them," I said, and it was not myself speaking. The Devil had entered into me too. I saw only the hunger in her eyes and I wanted her eyes to devour me, her body to enfold me, wanted to give myself to her because I was her master, as a strong swimmer gives himself to the sea.

The sun and the seals were our witness, and afterwards, as I lay face downwards in the grass, I thought how it was in this same Bay of

Seals, face downwards, with the woman and child beside him, that they had found the captain of *The Guiding Light*. Through all my childhood I had heard that story: how he was a thickset, black-bearded man, in a dark blue coat with brass buttons that the sea had not yet tarnished, and with one blue eye, the other having been torn out by the rocks. And now it was my turn to lie prone in the Bay of Seals with a woman beside me, and at the thought a great shudder ran through me, so that Agnes asked, "What is it?" But she had never heard the tale, so I said it was the tail-end of ecstasy and rolled over on my back while her fingers traced patterns on my face, and for vanity I asked her, "Am I better than Owen?" And at once I knew it was a mistake.

Her fingers slid off my face and she sat up slowly, gathering up her hair which lay over her shoulders like bright weed. "Much, much better," she said. "And now, Davy, you have shown me that I am a weak and worthless woman, and for my sake you must go away."

And because I am a god-fearing man and knew that I had sinned in taking my cousin's wife, and because I knew there was no future for me with Agnes so long as Owen was alive, I went like Owen before me to Cardiff, and it was six months before Porthfynnon saw me again.

When I came back on a week's holiday it was October. Owen and Agnes came to supper the night that I arrived, and I noticed how Agnes's smooth face looked fuller under her piled-up hair. There was a new contentment about her and it maddened me, for I had expected to find her as lean and hungry-looking as Aunt Miriam said I was. Instead I was forced to recognize that "Out of sight, out of mind" was as true as "Absence makes the heart grow fonder," only the first was true of Agnes and the second, despite every distraction, even physical exhaustion, had become increasingly true of me.

Agnes was busy with weaving, but I did not go to watch her at her loom because I did not trust myself to see unmoved those white hands moving the bright wools of the tapestry patterns, and her helpers and pupils might have observant eyes. So I sat and talked to Aunt

Miriam, who was now full of praise for Agnes, went out a couple of times with Owen and Uncle Robert in the boat, and spent the rest of the time tramping the familiar cliff paths. I was on the cliffs south of Porthfynnon the day of the great storm.

The weather had been working up to something all week. There was an unnatural stillness in the air, broken on Thursday by little tremors of wind so faint they were barely discernible. By Friday morning it was blowing a good gale. None of the fishing-boats went out that day. Grey clouds scudded low over the sea, which heaved itself into long, powerful, sluggish-looking waves that surged ceaselessly shorewards and shattered against the cliffs in a tempest of thunder and spray.

By dinner-time the wind had reached Force Eight and was still rising. Aunt Miriam said I was crazy to go out, but something in me responded to the thrill of the storm and I went despite her. Two miles south of Porthfynnon, the grey clouds came down in rain. The rain was like big needles. I put my head down and turned for home when, above the scream of the wind and the drumming of the rain on my oilskins, I heard a tremendous crash. Instinctively I looked seawards. At first all was rain and spray in an early dusk, but then I made out the great swirl of white water about the Abbot, and at the edge of it a dark but unmistakable shape.

There was a ship on the Monks — a fair-sized vessel. More than that I could not make out, for she had no lights, fired no distress flares, and gave no sign of life. Fortunately for me, two other men glimpsed her also in the driving rain and the murk, and so they testified at the enquiry, or it would have gone badly for me. One of them was a van driver on the road from Fishguard to Porthfynnon; the other was the coastguard in his look-out, which is why I heard the double boom of the maroons to call out the lifeboat while I was still running and stumbling back to give the alarm. I was nearer to the lifeboat-station than to the village. Immediately I turned about, thinking I might help or at least watch the launching, with Uncle Robert and Owen among the crew.

When I reached the lifeboat-station, the first-comers were just arriving. Jack Davies, the motor-mechanic, was already in his oilskins and checking engines that he knew to be perfect. Frank Evans, the bowman, was pulling his kapok life-jacket over his head. At that moment a car stopped with a jerk and Uncle Robert and Owen fell out, followed by Mike Edwards, the second coxswain. When he saw me, Uncle Robert's face lit up.

"Davy! We're a hand short—you can come with us. Take Bob Hunter's oilskins there on that peg. He's had to go into Haverfordwest, and with weather like this I'd sooner have my full crew aboard. There'll be work for all of us tonight."

In less time than it takes to tell, we had manned the lifeboat: eight yellow-oilskinned figures with life-jackets pulled over our heads. Someone pushed out the chocks and we held on tightly as the *Margaret Freeling* hurtled down her rollered slipway, gathering speed like a fairground switchback, until she hit the water in a shower of spray. Her engines came to life at once and sent her heading towards the storm and the open water outside the shelter of the bay.

Never have I seen a sea like it. The waves seemed housetop high, great sliding walls of water up which we climbed and climbed. Then for a few seconds the gale screamed and whistled across us, drenching everything in icy spray, before the boat plunged vertically as if down a lift-shaft and the steep, ever-steeper climb began again. Sometimes the boat leaned so far back on her beam ends it seemed she must capsize. Sometimes, before the top of the climb was reached, the wave itself toppled and broke. Cascades like Niagara thundered vertically down upon the *Margaret Freeling*, as though they meant to sink her there and then.

But our lifeboat was a stoutly built vessel, for all she was only forty-two feet long. The *Margaret Freeling*'s hull was buoyant as the English oak and Canadian pine she was made of; she was self-righting even if she did capsize. And a stouter-hearted crew never sailed her: I looked round at the faces grim under their sou'westers. Second coxswain Mike Edwards was at the wheel; I could see him peering ahead through his clear-screens while Uncle Robert checked the position of the wreck. Jack Davies and his brother Bryn, the motor-mechanics, were listening to their diesels, despite the scream of the wind and the thunder of the sea. Frank Evans, the bowman, never took his eyes from Uncle Robert's face, as though to anticipate every command relating to anchor, winch, or line-throwing pistol. And Owen and I and Emrys Rees, the three deck-hands, leaned forward, sheltering as best we could.

At a command from Uncle Robert our searchlight shone out over the water, illuminating the smooth cruel side of a great wave. Then, as we breasted it, I saw away to starboard a boiling and eddying of water in all directions, and a sharp black pinnacle of rock. I knew then that we had reached the Abbot and his Monks, and there in the midst of them loomed the dark mass of the wreck.

I noticed once again that there were no lights on board her. Presumably her electricity had failed. Yet even so, there should have been handlamps to signal—if there was anyone left alive on board. But that was nonsense. A ship that size must carry a crew of twenty or thirty. They would not all have taken to the boats. It would be madness in such weather. Better to stay aboard and take their chance. When our signals remained unanswered, Uncle Robert tried the loud-hailer, but we were not near enough for his voice to carry, for still no answer came.

"No sense trying to get a line aboard her if there's no one to secure it," Frank Evans said brusquely. He looked again at that wild water and added, "Even if we could."

It was in all our minds that the situation was impossible; we could do nothing except stand by and wait for the seas to abate and the dawn to dispel the darkness, but we said none of this aloud. It was in our minds also that once before the Porthfynnon lifeboat had had to abandon a wreck, and I know it was most of all in Uncle Robert's. He had his grandfather's dishonour to wipe out.

"We'll go round to windward of her and drop down on our anchor," he ordered quietly. "That should bring us under her bows."

The manoeuvre sounded simple, but we knew as well as he did that it was both dangerous and difficult. To drop down on the anchor means to approach from the windward side, allowing the lifeboat to drift towards its objective on a cable attached to the dropped anchor and controlled by the boatswain at the winch. Frank Evans was already taking up position in the bows as the *Margaret Freeling* turned into the wind to make a sweep that would bring her round to windward of this lampless, silent vessel. Suddenly disaster struck.

We had only just begun scaling one of those walls of water when Frank Evans shouted. There was a note in his voice I had never heard before. We were in the trough of the wave and at an angle, and already the succeeding wave, a monster overtopping it, was beginning to curl and break. We were all on our feet, clinging to anything within reach, as the double wave crashed down upon us and the deck tilted sharply. I glimpsed Frank Evans, his mouth still open, step back and disappear as the sea swept his words away, and then I had no handhold, no deck beneath me, no air in my lungs, my chest was bursting, and for an instant I caught sight of the lifeboat's hull, white-painted below the water-line, and knew that we had capsized.

In that same instant I also filled my lungs, and with oxygen came calmness. It was useless to struggle in such a sea. All I could do was to give myself as utterly as I had once done to Agnes, as I had done a thousand times to this element, as — at the end when there is no more hope in him — a man may give himself to death.

The great surges bore me up. I snatched air when I could, and saw with horror that the waves were carrying me straight onto the Monks. I prayed then that I might drown before being dashed to pieces. I closed my eyes and tried to will myself to die. And at that moment one of the lesser waves picked me up quite gently and tossed me sprawling, spewing, gasping, onto the deck of the vessel whose crew we had come to save.

I clung, too shaken to realize it was wood I was clinging to, until coherent thought returned. I got to my knees. I was bruised, but nothing seemed broken, and for the moment I was in comparative safety on the wreck. At that moment a tremendous sea broke over her stern, I felt her shudder through all her length, heard a creaking and groaning, and realized how precarious my safety was.

I also realized that the decks were slippery with seaweed, that green hairlike wrack that is usually found on rocks. My hands touched wood where I should have expected metal. There was something very odd about this ship. I shouted, but there was no answer. Indeed, I scarcely heard my own voice. Gingerly I began to move forward and my feet tangled in knotted rope. I fell heavily and the rope was all about me, like rigging stretching away towards the listing side of the ship. Like the deck, it was weed-encrusted. I jerked sharply, and as a result of my puny efforts the once-stout manila broke. Rottenness and decay were everywhere. I was beginning to be frightened by now, not of death, not of drowning or of being dashed to pieces, but of something I could not name. The planking of the deck was so rotten that when I stamped a long sliver broke. Yet the seas breaking over the vessel had less effect than I did. I began to wish that another wave would sweep me off.

But curiosity and self-preservation both prompted me to enter a doorway which I now noticed on my right. Here at least I should be out of the wind and spray, for a steep wooden stair led downwards to the still intact forequarters of the ship. There was a faint light at the bottom of the stairway; it shuddered with every blow upon the hull, and I saw that the light came from an old-fashioned storm-lantern hung on a bracket. So the vessel had some crew after all.

The light showed me another doorway, through which a stronger light glowed. I knocked; then, thinking this might pass for one of the storm's noises, I called out: "Is anybody there?"

Silence.

I could see that the cabin was furnished. Reassured, I stepped boldly inside—and stopped short, transfixed by the tableau before me. I see it in my mind's eye yet.

At the big table facing me a man was sitting, his head buried in his folded arms. He was black-haired and wore dark clothing. As my shadow fell across the lantern-light, he wonderingly raised his head. He had a square-cut black beard in a style no longer in fashion, and there were brass buttons on his double-breasted coat. One bright blue eye glared at me, the other was an empty socket. His face was nothing but a skull.

"Who are you?" His voice was deep and resonant.

I felt myself sweat with fear.

"Davy Jones from the *Margaret Freeling,* sir — the lifeboat — "

"The lifeboat, eh? One hundred years too late."

Even before he said it, I knew him: the captain of *The Guiding Light.* Had I not heard of him through all my childhood, with his one blue eye, his square-cut black beard, and his coat whose brass buttons the sea had not yet tarnished? And now he was before me in his cabin, on board a ship which a century ago had been smashed to pieces, and he himself buried in our churchyard, out of the sound of the sea. But supposing that I was as dead as he was and that in death all men are equal, I answered him boldly: "It's not rescue I'm bringing you, Captain. I'm the sole survivor. The *Margaret Freeling* capsized not half an hour ago."

"The sole survivor," he said. "You hear that, Nancy? I promised you this when that lifeboat put back into port and abandoned us a hundred years ago."

It was then that I noticed the woman sitting on the sofa under the porthole. She had her back to me, and her hair flowed down over her shoulders like Agnes's. Gold it was too, but there was a greenness about it as though it were tarnished with weed. When she turned her head, I saw that her eyes were wide and staring, but her face too was a skull.

"What's the use?" she said. "Capsized or cowardly, so far as we're concerned it's all one. There's no help coming. We should have gone with the others."

I asked the captain: "Where are your crew?"

"They've abandoned ship," he said. "When the lifeboat turned back the first mate gave the order. They must all be drowned by now."

"So there are only you two?"

"Three," he corrected me.

I saw then that the woman had a child, in her arms.

"We shall wait for the end in this cabin," he went on firmly, "as we waited for it once before — the three of us and John Stallworthy, the second mate. He survived, you remember. You can have Stallworthy's place."

He pointed to a seat at the table opposite the woman. She had bent her head to the child and her hair mercifully hid her face. I could not get out of my mind those staring eyes that the women of Porthfynnon had been unable to close.

The ship shuddered as another wave struck her. Seeing me flinch, the captain said grimly, "We shan't have long to wait."

"What happened?" I asked.

"What is happening now. The waves smashed her to pieces. After the lifeboat put back, we knew there was no more hope. We sat and listened to her breaking up. Nancy here was praying — " And above the child's head, I saw the woman's lips move.

"She might as well have saved her breath," the captain went on. "It was not God's will we died, but man's. When the coxswain of the lifeboat put back to port, he signed our death-warrant."

I said, "He had to think of his own crew."

"Yes, he saved his own skin and left Nancy and Hannah to perish."

"He didn't know there was a woman and child on board."

"Why so quick to defend him?"

"He was my great-grandfather," I said.

The captain's one blue eye was fixed unwinkingly upon me. He went on: "I said that I didn't pray, but I prayed that I might have vengeance on that lifeboat, if I had to wait a hundred years. And a hundred years I have waited. After this I can rest."

I should have felt sorry for him if I had not thought of Uncle Robert and Owen, and Frank Evans falling backwards, and the rest of the lifeboat's crew.

"If you're responsible for what happened to the lifeboat," I said, "may you burn in Hell forever."

His blue eye glared at me. "Shut your mouth! You're going to live to tell the tale."

"What do you mean?" I asked, for I still believed I was a ghost, as they were.

"When she breaks up," he said, "you're going to get ashore. John Stallworthy did and you're in Stallworthy's place. Besides, it's fitting: one man from *The Guiding Light* and one from the lifeboat. 'An eye for an eye'—isn't that how the Good Book has it?"

"Perhaps, but there is nothing good about this."

"Well said, man. There is nothing good about drowning, nor about knowing that you're going to drown. Soon after the lifeboat turned back the main and mizzen masts went the way of the foremast, and shortly afterwards she broke her back. But this forequarter still held—she was stoutly built—and still the seas swept over us. Then there was a fearful crash and the storm-lantern went out. We could hear the water and soon we could feel it—it came pouring down that stairway and swirled about our knees. I took Nancy in my arms and Hannah. We stayed on our feet as long as we could. Suddenly there were waves around us. I felt the wind. A balk of timber struck us. My grip relaxed, and after that they were gone."

There was so much anguish in his voice that I shuddered in sympathy, but I hardened my heart and said:

"Captain—I don't know your name, but that does not matter—you have been dead a hundred years, but tonight you have risen from the churchyard where you were given Christian burial, and because of you seven men are newly dead. Seven men who never harmed you, whose only connection with you is that they are the crew of the present lifeboat. Do you intend to rise again in another hundred years and take fresh vengeance?"

"Not if all goes as it should tonight."

"And if it doesn't?"

"If it doesn't, if any but you survive, I shall rise again down all the centuries so long as time shall endure."

"Amen to that," the woman said quietly, and turned her skull face towards me as she spoke. "For the sake of my child, my husband, I have risen from the dead for vengeance. If it is not complete, I shall rise from the dead again."

The child in her arms stirred, lifted her head, and I cried "No!" with a loud voice because I could not bear to see those empty eye-sockets, those milk teeth. . . . And at that moment the light went out.

There was a fearful crash and I could hear the sound of water. A moment later I felt it around my legs. The wind was on my face, the water was already waist high. My feet went from under me and I was swimming in the open sea.

The gale was blowing itself out. I was aware of that even while I fought to keep my head above water. The sea heaved menacingly, but the waves were no longer house-high. Dawn was breaking, and I could hear the thunder of surf against the land. I gave myself to the sea and the sea took me upon her bosom and somehow I too was borne towards the shore. There was no sign of the wreck. The Abbot and his Monks were a swirling mass of white water, but it was empty. I saw no living thing except a cormorant.

It was while I was in this state of exhaustion, almost stupor, knowing that I could never keep afloat long enough to reach the land yet not greatly caring, that I heard the last sound I ever expected to hear. Across the waste of the waters, carried by the wind, long-drawn-out but unmistakable, came the sound of a human cry.

I trod water, struggling to look around me. To my right I made out a dark object among the waves. With the last of my strength I swam towards it. It was a piece of driftwood and clinging to it was a yellow-oilskinned figure with a life-jacket. As I too caught hold of the wood he raised his head for a moment. It was Owen.

I do not know how he had survived, but then I do not know how I survived either. Owen was pretty far gone, but already the sea seemed less hostile because there were two of us, and the land was coming nearer all the time. I could make out the indentations of the coastline, and I knew that if we could only be swept ashore in some sheltered bay there was a chance we might escape being dashed to pieces, and two at least of the crew of the *Margaret Freeling* would live to tell the tale.

Two of us! And one small piece of driftwood. And with that I heard again the captain's voice: "If any but you survive, I shall rise again down all the centuries, so long as time shall endure." Other lifeboats from Porthfynnon would be in peril, called out to phantom wrecks. Other women and children would be widowed, orphaned. And the woman's voice said in my ear: "I have risen from the dead for vengeance. If it is not complete, I shall rise from the dead again."

I looked at Owen. They had promised me I should be the sole survivor, and from the look of him that might well be so. Only an exceptional physique could have endured as long as he had, but it was obvious he could take very little more. With each lurching wave I expected to see his grip slacken, yet each time he managed to hang on. I thought of the captain of *The Guiding Light* and his threat, and I began to pray that Owen, my cousin whom I loved as a brother, might never come safe to shore; Owen who had married Agnes, my Agnes, who would never look at me so long as Owen was alive.

I do not know whether I unbalanced him or whether a wave did it for me, but suddenly one hand-hold had gone. He was kept afloat now only by the piece of driftwood under one armpit. I leaned over and he thought it was to grasp him — I saw the gratitude in his eyes. And then I pushed him in the chest and he went backwards all in one piece, as though he were stiff already, and he opened his eyes and smiled past me, not seeing me, and I heard him say "Agnes." Thereafter the sea filled his mouth.

So I came slowly to land, the sole survivor, not worried overmuch because it was promised me I should be, and because I should bring happiness to Agnes once her first sorrow was over, and Agnes was the only thing in the world for me. So, still clinging to my driftwood that had been Owen's, as someday I should cling to Owen's wife, I was washed up at last, quite gently, among the smooth grey boulders and the sand in the Bay of Seals.

The day was a day of mourning in Porthfynnon, but I knew none of it until the late afternoon, when I rose from my bed in the unaccustomedly silent house to which they had taken me and came stumbling down the stairs. There was a strange woman in Aunt Miriam's kitchen, a Mrs. Bishop, who cried out at sight of me.

"Ah, Davy, you shouldn't be up. The doctor said you were to stay in bed and he'd call again this evening."

"Damn the doctor," I said. "Where is everyone? Where's Aunt Miriam?"

Mrs. Bishop put a hand to her mouth and stared at me as if I were raving. "She's down on the shore with the rest."

"And Agnes — Mrs. Owen?"

"She'll be down there too."

"Right, then, Mrs. Bishop. I'll join them."

"A cup of tea at least before you go."

"Thank you, but it's time enough I've wasted already. How long have I been here?"

"They found you at first light this morning. Oh, Davy, what happened, man?"

"The lifeboat capsized."

"But about the wreck — the wreck that never existed? Jim Rhodes, the coastguard is almost beside himself. One minute he swears he saw it, and the next says he must be mad."

"There was a wreck, Mrs. Bishop. I saw it."

The woman said fervently, "Praise be!" and I wondered if she would be quite so loud in her praise if I told her about *The Guiding Light*.

"I must run and tell Jim Rhodes —" she was taking off her apron — "he's had reporters round him all day like flies round a tray of offal at midsummer. There's no trace of the wreck, see."

"She broke up."

Mrs. Bishop was hanging on my words, no doubt thinking of what the newspapermen would tip her, but she could give as well as get.

"There's two men coming down from London," she volunteered. "To hold an enquiry. Oh, Davy, you'll have to give evidence."

Dazed though I was, I realized that the truth would never be believed, so I said: "There's nothing I can tell them. The ship broke up in the night."

"But there's no one come ashore from her." She meant dead bodies.

"They came ashore a hundred years ago," I said, and I passed out of the house, leaving her staring after me as if my wits had gone.

The village street was deserted save for a dog lying unsleeping on a doorstep. He lifted his muzzle and whined as I went by. I was not the master he was waiting for. I saw then that it was Emrys Rees's dog. Everywhere blinds were drawn. The general-store-cum-post-office had its shutters up. Faintly the sound of hammering could be heard: Morgan the carpenter at work on seven coffins. There should have been an eighth for me.

When I reached the cliffs, it was as though the whole village was assembled. I saw that they had towed the lifeboat in and were now unloading something in yellow oilskins on a stretcher. I looked away and saw Aunt Miriam.

She was standing with a group of other women. I went up to her and spoke. She turned round as if a ghost had touched her.

"Davy! You ought to be in bed."

"My place is here," I told her. "Have they—have they come ashore?"

"Robert has. Oh, Davy, his face! The rocks had battered it." She heard my silence and said in answer: "Owen hasn't come in yet."

I saw that the mother of the Davies boys was weeping. Emrys Rees's young wife looked old. Michael Edwards's father and brother were wading out towards the lifeboat, as if they knew who the canvas stretcher bore.

"And Agnes?" I asked Aunt Miriam. "Where's Agnes?"

She pointed a little way apart. "She neither speaks nor stirs. Unnatural it is. Go to her, Davy. Perhaps for you she will."

Agnes was standing on a slight rise and looking seaward. She was like the figurehead of a ship. I approached her from behind and put my heart in my voice to say her name—"Agnes."

She spun round, and the hope died in her eyes. "Davy! You sounded just like Owen."

I found there was nothing I could say. She had resumed her seaward gazing and was a thousand light-years away.

I said, "I'm sorry, Agnes."

I think she inclined her head.

I went on desperately, "Don't weep, heart's treasure. I still love you. I'd do anything to show how much."

"Be quiet," she said, not turning. "This is no time to talk of love. Oh, you will tell me I began it, that day in the Bay of Seals. But I did not know what love was then — it was Owen who has taught me, and I feel I am in some way responsible for his death. Ridiculous you will say it is, but I know better. It is I who have brought him to this."

I put from me the thought of Owen clinging to life and a piece of driftwood.

"You're talking wildly. Come away, Agnes. Come home."

"Not without Owen."

"But it's getting dark."

"The darkness in my heart is greater."

"We cannot stay here all night."

"*You* need not stay," she said indifferently. For an instant she turned her face to mine, and I saw her eyes, as grey now and still as the sea in winter. And a hundred thousand times as cold.

I wanted to tell her about the captain of *The Guiding Light,* and how, by enabling him to fulfil his revenge I had laid him to rest forever, but instead my voice said for me: "Owen spoke your name before he died."

She wept then, and women came around and surrounded her, and Aunt Miriam led her away. I heard one of the women say, "High time too, and her in her condition," and another answered, "It'll be a comfort to her, the child."

I knew then that I should never lie again with Agnes, that Owen's child would lie forever between her and me. The realization rushed over me like a black cloud of unknowing, and I fell unconscious where I stood.

There is little more to say. They held the funeral in the village church with six coffins only, for Owen never came ashore. I stood alone in my pew, and the whole village looked at me, wondering why I should be saved. Afterwards the six coffins were buried in the churchyard, and space left against the wall for Owen who had no grave. It was a generous space—I measured it. There was room for me as well, and so I told Aunt Miriam, who said gently, "We'll see," as if talking to a child or a half-wit. Everyone talked that way to me.

The men from London came down and conducted their enquiry, but I was not called to give evidence. Instead they called Jim Rhodes the coastguard, and the man who had been driving a van on the road from Fishguard to Porthfynnon. The enquiry concluded that a tragic false alarm had called the lifeboat out, but added that though the two men had been mistaken, they had been mistaken in good faith, and that anyone glimpsing the Abbot and his Monks in certain storm conditions might think he made out the outlines of a wreck.

I talk to everyone I meet about the captain of *The Guiding Light*, but they do not believe a word of it. The doctor comes cheerily to see me and says he will soon have me out and about and back at the swimming and fishing, but he talks a long time with Aunt Miriam and looks grave as he goes away. Agnes I never see, for she does not come near me, though I catch sight of her now and then, carrying her ripening belly proudly before her as she awaits the birth of Owen's son.

But it is all as if in a dream—a dream that will end shortly, somewhere around the time of the shortest day, when, like John Stallworthy one hundred years before me, I shall slip quietly out of life.

Aunt Miriam has promised that I shall lie beside the empty grave for Owen, in the lee of the churchyard wall, and I wait calmly for Death to gather the gleanings which he so unaccountably let fall.

Only when the wind blows from the south-west do I become restless, and walk down to the shore to watch the waves come in, in case they should be bringing Owen, who was like a brother to me. More than anything in this world I want to feel his hand in mine, strong and warm and vital, to hear the ring of his voice, but though I watch and wait the tides ebb and flow and never bring him, though their surges send a fever through my blood.

I know then that for those who are of the tribe of Cain there is no peace in this world. There is no peace anywhere for me, except the peace I shall find in our sheltered flower-bright churchyard, out of the sound of the sea.

This book has been printed by Worzalla Publishing Company, Stevens Point, Wisconsin, by Sheet-fed Offset on 70 # White Regular Flambeau Offset. The type is Baskerville, composed by Fox Valley Typesetting, Menasha, Wisconsin. The book was Smyth sewn and bound by Worzalla.